STEPCHILD ON THE VISTULA
LUGUS PUBLICATIONS

D1202928

STEPCHILD ON THE VISTULA

S. SIMCHOVITCH

LUGUS

Canadian Cataloguing in Publication Data

Simchovitch, Sam
  Stepchild on the Vistula

ISBN: 0-921633-53-X

I. Title.

PS8537. I53S84 1994   C813'.54   C94-931074-3
PR9199.3.S55S84 1994

© S. Simchovitch 1994
Cover Art by Ernest Raab

FOR FRAIDLE WITH LOVE

ACKNOWLEDGEMENTS

I would like to acknowledge the kind assistance of Mr. Ted Wood in revising this manuscript. Thanks are also due to Elie Wiesel, for permitting me to quote from his letter published in the Yiddish edition of this novel, and to Ernst Raab for the fine cover drawing. The following friends contributed generously towards the publication of this edition: Joseph B. and Olyn Horwitz of Holywood, Florida; also Izzy and Batya Kirshenbaum, the late Bernard and Ruth Cooper, Victor and Renee Topper, and Irv and Helene Newman, all of Toronto.

INTRODUCTION

At daybreak, on Wednesday, August 19, 1942, a detachment of German Einsatz troops, and their auxiliaries, broke into the ghetto of Otwock (Otvotzk), 28 kilometres south of Warsaw. Shouting and shooting indiscriminately, they herded over eight thousand Jews behind the nearby railway station and transported them in freight trains to Treblinka, where all of them were murdered. The remainder of more than four thousand hidden Jews—men, women and children—were afterwards shot and buried in several mass graves in the city. Only a handful managed to escape, and even fewer—to survive. This was the end of the Jewish community of Otwock and its surroundings. Here the Jews had lived for many generations beside their Polish neighbours, building and developing the city and the whole region into a beautiful resort known all over Poland.

Stepchild on the Vistula is the story of one young Otwock Jew—Nohum Freidowicz—from Swiderska Street, in the poor, workingman's section of the city. His childhood and coming of age are told against the background of the vibrant and colourful life of the Otwock Jews, as it has remained vividly in my memory since I left the place, at the age of eighteen, in the first week of World War II.

The original version of this book was written and published in Yiddish in Toronto, 1992. It had won the 1993 award for Yiddish Literature of the Book Committee of the Jewish Federation of Greater Toronto, and it was acclaimed by many critics as an enlightening portrayal of Jewish life in Poland before the onset of the Holocaust.

S. Simchovitch
Toronto

Chapter 1
THE HOME

Nohum was several months old in 1921 when the Red Army overran Poland and reached the outskirts of Warsaw. Sobien, where he was born, was hit by artillery fire. Its inhabitants fled for their lives to the fields outside the shtetl. It was then that Moshe-Avrohom, Nohum's father, decided to move to Otwock, a city on the rail-line south of Warsaw. Otwock had begun to develop into a resort town for the healthy and the sick alike. Moshe-Avrohom with his wife, Itte, and the two children, Nohum and Shaindel, reached there on a peasant's cart with their belongings and sewing machines. He rented an apartment in a house in the Jewish section, between the railway tracks and the bazaar. He put up anew his boot-stitching shop in the larger front room. The smaller back room became the living quarters for the family. This back room had a view of the courtyard and there the sun seldom penetrated. Inside the room stood the separate beds of father and mother along the wall leading to the window. The kitchen stove was opposite the beds and, near it, a low wooden cabinet with a pail and bowl for washing hands. Between this cabinet and the door stood a closet with carved doors and drawers.

With the approach of winter, Moshe-Avrohom insulated the family room from the cold. He shut the door to the courtyard and filled its cracks with rags and straw. He took apart the closet and reassembled it in front of the door to protect the household. He placed a small iron stove in the middle of the room. The tin flues stretched into a chimney above the kitchen. On cold days, the stove would glow with burning coals and its pipes carried the lovely warmth all through the house. Itte gave birth to two daughters in the room behind the shop. The first, Tema, was a swarthy girl with an elongated face and fine features resembling her father's; the other, Rochel, a year and a half younger, was of fair complexion and had yellowish hair, similar to her mother's.

After a three year interval, Moshe-Avrohom then fathered a second son. He was named Godel, and he was a dark-haired baby with a delightful little smile. Since times were more prosperous, Moshe-Avrohom celebrated the arrival of his second male child with the traditional Friday night party. Sewing machines in the shop were covered with bedsheets and tables were set with food and drink for friends and neighbours.

The one-room home was soon filled with childrens' cries and voices. They got sick, had bouts of scarlet fever, measles and smallpox, but they recuperated (thanks to The One Above). When they did get sick, Itte would not rest but was on guard, day and night. In addition to the doctor, she would bring in someone familiar with incantations against the Evil Eye. When a child was high with fever, then she would dare to pour out her lament before the Almighty behind the curtain of the Holy Ark in the House of Study. Thus she saved all her infants from the clutches of the Angel of Death.

Most of all, Itte watched over her firstborn son, Nohum. He was a gentle, frail child, prone to many ailments. He suffered from eye inflammation; scarlatina; measles. Due to his enlarged tonsils he often came down with colds. Itte feared that those colds would, (God forbid) develop into pneumonia. She was aware that her husband's father had died of tuberculosis while still in his forties. Moshe-Avrohom, broad-shouldered and sturdy though he was, had inherited a deep, hollow cough which often frightened her. Therefore she watched the boy more than the other children. In cold weather, she dressed him warmly, putting a woollen toque and scarf around his head. When, in spite of all precautions he did catch cold, she rubbed his back with alcohol, and warmed his place in bed with a hot tea kettle. Sometimes she asked her husband to put cupping glasses on his back—the remedy was effective.

Most of her days Itte was busy with household chores, but sometimes she had to leave the children and help out at the counter, selling accessories to her husband's customers. Shaindel, her stepdaughter, whose mother had died at childbirth during the war, attended Polish school and could be of help only in the late afternoon after she had finished her homework. In the evening, when Shaindel put Nohum to bed, she would tell him stories of Polish kings and knights who fought the German Crusaders, or of the beautiful Queen Wanda who drowned herself in the Vistula and became a water-fairy.

On winter nights, Itte herself began to spin tales of her own childhood and youth, which were spent in a village near Lublin. Her father (may he rest in peace) was a village tutor and used to venture into far-off hamlets to teach children Hebrew prayers and portions from the Five Books. More than once he got lost in fields and woods, where robbers and wild animals roamed. Sometimes he was attacked by vicious country dogs, but (thank God) he always returned safely for the Sabbath and holidays.

A nasty snow storm might rage outside, but the room would be warm and cozy. Shaindel would be in the middle of a story, and Itte beginning to prepare the beds for her household. This was not an easy task; the room was cluttered and souls were already five, not counting mother and father. The best situated was Godel, the youngest, resting comfortably in his wooden crib in the middle of the room. The oldest, Shaindel, also slept by herself on a folding bed, while the two younger girls, Tema and Rochel, were squeezed into their mother's bed. Nohum slept with his father and loved to cuddle against his hairy chest and feel his warm breath. But when Moshe-Avrohom sometimes woke up in the middle of the night with heavy coughing, Nohum became frightened, until his father put him at ease, whispering in his ear reassuringly, "My little one, it's nothing, nothing..."

Nohum seldom noticed when his father went to bed and when he arose—Moshe-Avrohom used to be so busy in his workshop from early morning till late at night. He arose at dawn, opened the shutters, and recited the morning prayers. When Nohum woke up early, he used to see his father standing near the window, wrapped in his broad prayer shawl, with the large phylacteries on his head and arm, slowly rocking his body back and forth, like an unearthly being. Morning prayers over, Moshe-Avrohom entered the shop where he spent his entire day.

Only on Saturday mornings were he and his wife slow to rise. The children, in long nightshirts, scampered from bed to bed, tasting the Sabbath cookies their mother had baked the day before. Then Nohum loved to climb on his father and ride him like a pony. Skillfully his father would throw him back on the straw mattress, but Nohum mounted him again, calling, "Hetta-vio, hobby!" Moshe-Avrohom would throw him down again and, finally, close his strong arms around him. Nohum would feel his father's prickly beard against his face and hear him murmur, "My little fool, my dear one..."

When Sabbath was over, Moshe-Avrohom resumed his former demeanour—stern, reticent, ready for another week in his workshop.

Chapter 2
THE WORKSHOP

The workshop, unlike the dark and crowded back room, was large; here the sun shone brightly through the window and door panes from the morning until early afternoon. Beside the window were the two stitching machines—the low one, for light footwear, and the tall one, for boots. At the edge of both machines was a table with a wooden cutting board over which Nohum's father cut out the leather uppers of shoes and boots.

At the lower machine sat Itzhakel, the operator, a stout fellow with mocking eyes and a pitch-black shock falling over his forehead. Usually he hummed a leftist ditty to the rhythm of the whizzing machine:

> Snow fell over the night,
> Two youths marched side by side,
> They carried a hidden red band—
> Greetings for Soviet land...

On one occasion Moshe-Avrohom, bent over the outspread sheet of leather, reproached him quietly:

"Shut your mouth, Itzhakel. The walls have ears."

"I don't give a damn!"

Itzhakel laughed and began to hum another forbidden tune.

Since Nohum had begun to walk, he had loved to steal into his father's shop and observe everything that was going on. He especially enjoyed both Itzhakel's songs and his jolly disposition. There was also another apprentice, Leibush, who was a lanky lad with a pointed red nose and gaping mouth from which a few large yellowish teeth stared out.

Imagine him now sitting on a stool at the tall boot-machine, holding an upturned bootleg, covered with clay, which had to be turned over to its proper side. Leibush—struggling with the long double-leather bootleg, wiping the sweat from his forehead with his greasy hands. Itzhakel looking at him mockingly for a while, until he gets up, takes the bootleg from Leibush, and effortlessly

4

turns it to its proper state. Then with the black, shiny bootleg, rapping Leibush's head and laughing in his face:

"Blind mare, who gave birth to you, your father or mother?"

At the end of the shop, along the entrance to the back room, stood the wooden counter. Behind it were wall shelves stocked with hard and soft leather, shoe-nails, and shoemaker's accessories. When necessary, Nohum's mother came in from the room behind to sell the merchandise to the cobblers. Ruby-faced, with long blonde hair down to her shoulders, she now stands behind the counter weighing a pile of tiny nails for a tall Polish boot-maker, Gaiger, who speaks to her in Yiddish:

"Moshkovna, add a bit of nails. It's not nice to cheat a goy."

All his life in close proximity with Jews—neighbours, customers, and apprentices—Gaiger had learned to speak Yiddish fluently. He boasted that he knew by heart the Modeh Ani prayer that Jews recite every morning. Gaiger remained in the store for a while to chat with another shoemaker who had just entered with a bundle of leatherware under his arm.

"What's new, Shlomke?"

Gaiger taps the newcomer on the shoulder.

At ease, the two cobblers light hand-rolled cigarettes on the heated brick stove in the middle of the shop. There, Nohum is now busy throwing pieces of leather he has picked up from the floor, to see them glow in red and blue fire tongues.

"Away, little rascal! You'll burn down the place," the cobblers scold.

Nohum moves away from the stove toward the entrance door where he can gape at the glass panes ornate with strange wintry compositions. Soon the door opens and a white stretch of snow-covered street dazzles his eyes. From behind the counter his mother warns him:

"Nohumel! Away from the door! You'll catch cold again!"

In front of the closed door stands an elderly Jew with a broad, graying beard, deep sad eyes, and bent shoulders. Slowly he shakes off the snow from his fur hat and long dark coat and calls out plaintively:

"Good morning, dear Jews!"

Moshe-Avrohom greeted him.

"Good year to you, Reb Lozer!"

"Oh no, Moshe-Avrohom, do not call me Reb Lozer," said the

newcomer in a chant. "Call me Misery, Affliction, whatever you want, not Reb Lozer."

Itzhakel, bent over the machine, can hardly restrain himself from laughing and begins to hum a doggerel:

> Good Purim to all,
> Where I go, I fall;
> My beard is thick,
> My wife is sick ...

"Sing, sing, smart aleck," Lozer retorts. "As long as you are out of the dungeon, you may sing your witty songs." Itzhakel blushes; he is ready to respond, but notices Moshe-Avrohom's stern look and says no more.

Reb Lozer sat down on a stool beside the boot-machine and began to unpack the hot lunch he brought for his son Leibush.

"Mother sent you a hot meal, my jewel".

"She did a good thing, Father. I'm hungry," Leibush said as he grabbed the warm pot.

"Put on your cap! Don't eat with an uncovered head, like a peasant!" Lozer reproached his son. Leibush put on his cap and began to eat.

"Tell me, my son," Lozer said after a while, "tell me the truth: will you say Kaddish after me, when I am gone!"

"Yes, Father, I will," Leibush assured him, dipping a slice of bread in his soup.

"I don't trust you, goy! Would I not have lived to see what's become of you!" said Lozer, holding back his tears.

Lozer Shpeker was an old friend of Moshe-Avrohom, from his home town of Gora-Kalwaria, or Ger, in Yiddish.

"A pity on this Jew," Nohum heard his father say more than once. "All the misfortunes of the world had to come upon him."

"If there is no mazel, you shouldn't be born," Nohum's mother commented.

Lozer himself suffered from a heart-ailment, his wife was housebound with diabetes, and their only daughter was an old maid, still at home. In addition, Leibush, his good-for-nothing son, was not at all eager to learn a trade and earn a living. His days were spent in loafing and idling. He was busy in the evenings at the Workers' Union, where he joined a drama group which prepared public performances once or twice a year. It was at one of these productions that he was arrested and spent several months in jail. For his last bit of money, Lozer had to hire a lawyer to get the boy out of prison. Lozer would often come over to Moshe-Avrohom to pour out his bitter heart.

"Dear Moshe-Avrohom," he would say, "I cannot bear it anymore! The waters have reached up to here," he would indicate with his hand at the throat. "It remains only to make an end to myself, God forbid." Moshe-Avrohom would always set him at ease, help him with a word of consolation or a promissory note. After Leibush was released from prison, out of pity to Reb Lozer, Moshe-Avrohom agreed to accept the boy into his workshop.

"Hey you, Itzhakel ganef," Lozer spoke again, "tell me the truth, is your Workers' Union preparing another Purim shpil?"

"You mean our drama group?" the apprentice corrected him in a dignified tone. "Of course, we are working on a new spectacle. We have an artistic director from Warsaw."

"I tell you, in God's name," Lozer pointed his finger at the operator, "you should not allow my buffoon of a son to take part in it! I'll throw him out of the house like a dog, you hear, like a dog!" Lozer addressed both his son and Itzhakel. "Yes, Father, I promise. No more theatre," Leibush said to calm him.

It had been two years since Leibush starred in one of the performances that made him the talk of the town. Throughout that winter, the drama group of the Workers' Union prepared for the spring revue. They rehearsed each week, worked on costumes and set decorations, and hired a hall for the production. Meanwhile, participants as well as bystanders recited excerpts from the rhymed satirical sketches:

> Come here, Itche-Ber,
> Come, please, my dear.
> I will tell you something,
> You'll rejoice and sing:
> All the strikers—done away,
> No more strikers—hooray, hooray!
> Now all will study the Holy Torah,
> And dance only the horah.

One of the main actors was none other than Leibush. At the opening night, he wore a black Hasidic gaberdine and a fur hat, with a beard and earlocks attached to his face. He wiped his face with a long, red kerchief, moving to and fro over an open book, and declaiming his verses in a talmudic chant. Suddenly, two plainclothes policemen, armed with guns, broke into the hall. Panic ensued; the audience ran for the doors and windows. Only Leibush did not lose his head. He stood up straight in the middle of the stage, unfurled his red kerchief, and called in a pitched voice: "Long live the Revolution! Down with ..."

Leibush did not finish his slogan before the two detectives grabbed him and led him away to the police station. There, Heniek, the red-baiter on the staff, gave the boy a hefty beating, after which he lay on the plank cot for a day or two until he was transported, under guard, to the District Detention Centre in Warsaw.

Moshe-Avrohom thought more than once of these Jewish rebels who had begun appearing everywhere since the end of the war. In his youth, he too had doubts in matters of religious beliefs and practices. He also attended workers' meetings where strikes were discussed. However, after marrying, he began to work for himself, children were born and he had to provide for a family. Thus he remained in the fold—an observant Jew. But now, he reflected, this new generation, they respect neither Jewish law nor the rule of the land. And all of them—revolutionaries, agitators, orators. Only God knows what this tumult would bring forth for the Jewish people. But, on the other hand, the matter was not so simple. It could be that these insolent youngsters would achieve more than his own generation ... would gain a better life for the common folk, the working people ... These thoughts troubled Moshe-Avrohom again as he looked at Lozer, over the head of Leibush, who was eating his meal as if nothing mattered. Reading somehow Moshe-Avrohom's thoughts, Lozer said in a subdued voice: "Moshe-Avrohom dear, who knows what ruin these rascals will bring upon the world?"

Hearing this, Itzhakel puckered his face and began to recite aloud:

> Let all the world be destroyed.
> And we,
> Sabbath-holiday Jews,
> With illumined souls,
> Shall tread upon her ruins.

Chapter 3
SWIDERSKA STREET

All winter the streets of the Jewish quarter lay huddled in frost and snow. From the low chimneys rose thin columns of smoke, and from the doors that were hurriedly shut, a whiff of warm steam reached the passer-by.

In mid-March, the snow began to melt, filling the streets with puddles till the April sun dried them out. The inhabitants of the quarter sighed with relief—at last, the long, hard winter was over. Over the dusty pavements draymen now hurried with their carts and horses, their whips whistling in the air. Bagel sellers, with straw baskets full of baked goods, roamed the streets, calling aloud:

"Fresh bagels! Small egg matzos!"

The children, who spent all the winter months inside their dark, crowded homes, emerged eagerly to enjoy the outdoors. Towards evening, when they had returned from Heder or the Polish school, small groups formed to play cops-and-robbers, hide-and-seek, and other games. Quieter children played with small balls, buttons, and coins.

Nohum was less than five years old and not yet in Heder when he began to explore the lively stretch of Swiderska Street outside his father's boot-stitching shop. The first neighbour in the long two-storey dwelling was the grain merchant, Itchele Gliniker. Itchele and his wife, Gitel, had no children, and spent all their days in the store full of sacks of grain and oats, which they sold to the draymen to feed their horses. Only on Friday, in the afternoon, Itchele left the store for the Mikveh, to purify himself for the Sabbath. Early in the evening, the whole courtyard would listen, through the open window of his second floor apartment, to Itchele's slow and prolonged chanting of the Kiddush and the Sabbath meal songs.

Next to Itchele was the front and back room of Faivel the Shoemaker who had lived for some years in Palestine where he had owned a small farm. Eventually, he returned to Poland because the hot climate did not agree with his wife's health.

Faivel's next neighbour was the Amshinower (so named after his home town of Amshinow), a poor boot-stitcher with bloodshot eyes from working day and night at his sewing machine.

"This Jew has grown to his work stool," neighbours used to say. "He won't last long this way," they pitied him. In addition, the Amshinower was often embarrassed by his daughter, Tzipe, a wild, neglected girl who was never still, always running, jumping, and spouting all kinds of noises. In the middle of running, she would stop abruptly and begin to whirl and spin like a circus dancer. The children on the street encouraged her to show off her tricks. "Tzipe, spin around! Tzipe, bark like a dog," they asked and Tzipe gladly obliged. Sometimes Tzipe's father tore himself away from his stool to bring his daughter home. Then the whole block would stop to behold the spectacle of the Amshinower chasing his daughter. Nimble as a cat, she would dart from under his outstretched arms and disappear into a nearby courtyard. Humiliated and gasping, the Amshinower would retreat to his sewing machine by the window.

Passing the vaulted entrance to the courtyard, Nohum would proceed along the sidewalk to the other wing of the building. Here were a few more stores: a laundry and a cleaners, a sewing and notions store, another shabby boot-stitching shop, and, finally, the textile business of Itchele Einfeld, the owner of the whole building. Itchele was a tall, portly man with a long beard reaching his substantial belly. His thick eyebrows and stern look evoked fear in children—also in adults.

Here the street ended and Nohum did not dare to venture further. From afar he could see the train tracks that ran through the city and the white structure of the railway station. In the square, in front of the landlord's store, was a large water pump around which the draymen and porters congregated. These were husky and hardy Jews, in short cotton jackets, their faces and beards tainted with flour dust and sweat. Here they fed their horses, while they waited to unload the incoming freight trains and deliver the merchandise to stores and hotels all over the city.

Nohum crossed the narrow street to see what was going on on the opposite side of the block. On the corner was the small restaurant of Leibel Sane's, where the draymen and porters would come in to warm up with a shot of whiskey or a mug of beer. Next was a kerosene store, another small boot-stitching shop, and several living quarters with entrances from the street. In one of them lived the paper-bag maker with his wife and two sons. The furniture of their large room consisted of several wrought-iron bed-frames and a long wooden table at which the whole family worked at cutting and pasting the brown paper bags. Next to them was an open entrance to a staircase leading to an upper floor apartment, where the ritual slaughterer and his family resided.

A new chain of shabby, half-sunken, one-storey dwellings followed. The first few rooms were occupied by the egg merchant and his family. Next door lived the "Deaf Shoemaker," then the "Little Tailor," who patched and revamped all the neighbours' clothing. Further along, Godel the tinman inhabited two rooms. The walls of the first room which served as a workshop, were blackened from the soot of the coal furnace which he pumped to life with a big pair of bellows. On Friday afternoons, Godel scrubbed himself clean and put on his uniform of the 'Covenant Soldiers', a paramilitary unit of the Revisionists, who were preparing to fight both the British and the Arabs, to restore the Jewish kingdom in Palestine. Next to the tinman, in a half-sunken room, lived Zanvele the Shoemaker—a tiny, shrivelled cobbler with a little wife, several children, and an old mother. The last house on the block belonged to Menashe the Coachman, who was really a shoemaker, but got fed up with stooping over his workbench and acquired a droshky with a brown, muscular horse to ride all over the city.

In the corner, to the left of Menashe's house, a narrow street led to the bazaar and market place, and further on, to the town of Karczew. A few houses further, on the right side of Swiderska Street, began Gorna Street, lined with groves and villas, up to the Swider River and to the resort town of the same name.

The corner of Swiderska and Gorna was the site of puzzling assemblies, which Nohum witnessed several times. Suddenly, as if from nowhere, young men and women appeared, all with bare heads, short jackets, and work blouses. As they came together in a dense mass, one of them was lifted upon another's shoulders and would begin to speak aloud, while those around shouted slogans and clapped their hands. They then stood attentively and sang, in unison, a solemn song.

The demonstration lasted only a short while; the assembled soon dispersed in all directions, as if they had done something wrong or forbidden. Once, while retreating, someone managed to fling a tiny red cloth over the electricity wires above the street. For hours the little red banner, attached to a cord with a stone at its end, dangled overhead, until two policemen brought it down. At that moment, the street became paralyzed with fear; people kept indoors and apprentices remained silent at their workbenches and sewing machines. Only a few of the younger children, Nohum among them, dared to come out, curious to see how the mighty policemen were struggling to bring down the little flag from the wires above. Quietly, the children whispered to each other overheard stories of the "Reds" who were at war with the police and the government. If one of them were caught throwing such a little flag, he would have to spend many years in prison. When the policemen left, the whole street sighed with relief.

The most lively day of the week was Friday, when the weekly fair was held. Nohum was eager to accompany his mother on her Friday morning shopping-rounds to the bazaar and the market. The streets around the bazaar were crowded with pedestrians and horse-drawn carts. Black-caftaned Jewish merchants and housewives with straw baskets in hand were streaming to the bazaar from all sides.

Inside the bazaar, Itte first stopped at the bakery booths laden with freshly baked bread, hallahs, and a variety of pastries. Afterwards, she walked over to the butchers and fish mongers to buy meat and fish for the Sabbath.

Out of the bazaar, in the grove along Karczew Street, were stands and covered booths with shoddy shoes and clothing. Peasants and their wives gaped at the polished boots, tried on the garments, and bargained aloud. Nearby, a husky fellow spun a painted gambling wheel on which young men staked their money. Behind them was a brightly painted carousel which swirled around to the tunes of an accordion.

From here, Itte and Nohum crossed over to the open market place on the other side of the street. The place was cluttered with loaded carts with sacks of grain, potatoes, and wooden cages with live poultry. Housewives weighed and felt the screaming geese and chickens, parting their plumage to examine the fat. The fowl shrieked and cackled, horses neighed, pigs wheezed, and the sounds of animals and men mingled under the bright open sky of the day.

Loaded with food for the Sabbath, Itte, with Nohum at her side, took a shortcut home through the nearby grove. Here Nohum found new attractions, like gathering pine-cones and wild flowers. Tired and impatient, Itte held Nohum by the hand and implored him:

"Nohumel, my crown! A half a day is gone; I still have to prepare for the Sabbath."

At the edge of the grove, facing the street, stood a life-size statue of the Nazarene—a tall, lean figure with a short beard and a sad, elongated face. He held in his left hand a wooden cross, while his right arm was outstretched towards the street. On the wooden stairs leading to the statue, several women knelt in silent prayer. On Sundays, religious processions would sometimes descend from the church in the upper side of the town. The church bells would ring uncannily and men and women in their holiday best would pass by, singing in pensive voices.

Across the shrine were the two bridges over which the trains from Warsaw to Lublin rushed to and fro. Under the bridges people walked leisurely. Black droshkies with newly arrived passengers hurried by, and paper-boys shouted the daily headlines. From here, along the sidewalk beside the railway fence, was a short distance to the comforts of their familiar Swiderska Street.

Chapter 4
WINTER

With the passing of summer, when most of the out-of-town guests left the pensions and villas, an air of sadness descended upon the city. The faces of men and women in the Jewish quarter became serious: one had to provide the home with coal and wood for winter, prepare a few sacks of potatoes and some other provisions, or order shoes and boots for the children so they could attend school.

As soon as the colder weather set in, Nohum's mother began to worry about the well-being of her children, especially Nohum. Each time she let him outside, she made him put on an additional sweater and scarf, so he would not catch cold. But all her precautions were often in vain; the child came back exhausted, with glassy eyes and a sore throat. Itte touched his forehead to feel the temperature and exclaimed, "Woe is me! The child has a cold again!" Right away she undressed him and put him under the warm and soft comforter.

Now Shaindel came to Nohum's bedside to entertain her sick brother with stories she read in school. This time she was telling him a story about a poor girl, a seller of matches, who wandered all alone in the cold winter night. Nohum closed his eyes and saw the snowflakes falling endlessly in the faraway city. Doors and gates were shut; only through the windows many coloured lights glimmered in the dark. The poor girl shivered from cold and to warm herself, lit one match after another. The tiny flames flickered for a while and went out in the snow-whirl hardly warming her small, frozen hands.

"Pity the girl," Nohum said. "Was she frozen to death?"

"Yes," said Shaindel quietly.

"And the One Above didn't save her?" inquired Nohum.

"No," answered Shaindel.

"What happens when you die?" Nohum insisted.

"I don't know," said Shaindel. "They say that the souls of the good people enter the Garden of Eden, while the wicked ones end up in Gehenna."

Here Nohum's mother came over to put a dressing of heated salt around his neck.

14

"Why are you scaring the child?" she scolded her stepdaughter. "May it come upon all the desolate fields and woods, not on my little Nohum," she intoned while applying the warm compress around her son's neck.

Nohum fell back unto the soft cushion and with half-closed eyes observed his room. From the electric bulb that hung down from the ceiling, golden rays spread in all directions. The fire in the small winter stove in the middle of the room crackled and its pipes carried the lovely warmth over the room. Shaindel was now doing her homework at the small table beside the wooden closet that was already moved to the back door for the winter. From Father's shop in the front room, one could hear the hum of the sewing machines and the rapping of light hammers over the cut leather.

In the evening, Moshe-Avrohom closed the shop and came in to his family. He went over to Nohum, took his pulse, and said to his wife, "The child has a cold, he needs cupping glasses."

"Nu," answered Itte, "You are the father."

Right away Shaindel was told to run over to a neighbour for the container with the cupping glasses.

At first, Moshe-Avrohom rubbed Nohum's back lightly, while Itte stood beside him ready with a burning candle in her hand. He then lit a small stick, its tip covered with cotton, and put the flame into each glass before sticking it on the child's back. One by one, the round cupping glasses came upon Nohum's back, tightening it until it was hard for him to breathe.

Quiet till now, Nohum began to whimper, "It's enough, dear Father! I can't stand it!"

"It is already done," Itte comforted him. "To your health!"

She put out the candle and covered Nohum with the feather quilt. Now Nohum rested patiently until he was again uncovered and Father carefully pulled the cups from his back. Relieved, he lay quietly and soon fell asleep.

After a few days the cold was over and Nohum again began to venture into Father's shop from where he could observe the street. Outside, fresh snow had fallen on the ground and rooftops and children were rejoicing its arrival. Some pulled small wooden sleighs, others threw snowballs at each other.

In the low, run-down house across the street, Nohum could see Zanvele the cobbler sitting, as always, beside his low shoemaker's table at the front window. In that house lived Hinda, Zanvele's youngest daughter, a tiny red-haired girl with a freckled face. In summer, when the children played all day on the street, Hinda used to watch them from afar, afraid they would chase her away or poke fun at her. Only Nohum felt close to her and they often played together on the sidewalk beside their homes.

For several days Nohum looked in vain for Hinda until he learned that she had fallen ill with pneumonia. When the doctor finally arrived in a droshky, Nohum heard from his mother that the girl needed God's mercy. She was seriously ill.

A few days passed and nothing was heard of Hinda until one afternoon a bitter outcry came from the cobbler's home. A few neighbours ran into Zanvele's home and came out wringing their hands. "The child died!" they announced. "Blessed be the righteous Judge!"

The next day a dark horse-drawn cart arrived in front of Zanvele's home and two bearded men from the Holy Society brought out the small wooden coffin and placed it on the wagon. Alongside, wailing and sobbing, walked Zanvele, his wife and daughters and a few of the women neighbours. The funeral procession quickly disappeared into the nearby street on the way to the city's far-off cemetery. For a long time afterwards Nohum keenly felt the eerie mystery of death. Many unanswered questions distressed him: Why did Hinda have to die? He himself had been sick for nearly a week and yet got up healthy as before. For Hinda, it seemed God ordained she should die. Why? And what did it mean to die? Is it true, as they tell you, that the body is buried in the earth forever? However, the soul, he comforted himself, goes up to Heaven. Hinda's soul must surely have reached the Garden of Eden where everything is so bright and beautiful. Why, then, did her parents and sisters lament so bitterly when she was carried away?

The following spring, the children found, in the courtyard's vegetable garden, a fledgling sparrow that had fallen from its nest. For a while they occupied themselves with the helpless creature, trying to feed and revive it. Soon the bird fell silent and died. The children then arranged for a funeral. Standing around solemnly, they buried the bird in a corner of the garden and placed a stone over its grave.

During the burial, Nohum vividly remembered Hinda who was now lying, as this little bird, in her grave in the cemetery grounds. His heart was filled with a great sorrow and tears welled up in his eyes. He turned away and allowed himself to cry over the fate of his little red-haired friend.

Chapter 5
THE COURTYARD

Separated from the street by the two-storey brick structure, the large courtyard pulsated with its own life and bustle. The boss in the yard was Leibel, the adopted son of Itchele Einfeld, the owner of the building. He was totally devoted to his parents, Itchele and Simele, collecting the rent from the sixteen tenants and keeping the building and the courtyard in order. Under Itchele's tutelage, Leibel grew up to be very pious and fearful of Heaven. He was undersized and lean, with a sparse yellow beard, always bubbling with excitement, as if he felt God's presence at hand. "O-va-va," he used to mumble to himself, "happy are the eyes that behold God's wonders. O-va-va..."

Whenever Leibel came across Nohum, he patted him on the head, then bent down to him and began his exhortation:

"Be a Jew, my child. It's good and wonderful to be a Jew, a servant of the Almighty."

Before Passover, when the mud puddles in the unpaved yard began to dry up, Leibel began to bring the neglected place in order. He was helped by the janitor, Horonzik, a Pole, already in his seventies, who had worked there for many years. Horonzik was familiar with all the tenants and their families. On Saturday morning, he hurried from household to household to kindle the stoves on which the Sabbath meals were warmed up. For this service, he was generously rewarded with slices of hallah or cake, and portions of chicken or gefilte fish for himself and his family, which lived somewhere, on the city's outskirts.

With Horonzik, Leibel inspected the yard and together they began to repair its fence, sheds and lockers. Meanwhile the great pre-Passover commotion had begun. Women carried pieces of furniture into the yard to clean and scrub them. Men were busy airing the holy books to ensure that no leavened crumbs remained in them. The books were laid out on the ground in rows, so the spring wind would ventilate their yellowish pages. Leibel, watching his books, enlightened Nohum: "Study, Nohumel, study God's word. Serve Hashem with joy, as it is written, 'all my bones

17

speak to the Lord'. Ay, ay, Master of the Universe, pity Thy holy sheep."

Right after Passover, Leibel began to repair the fence of the small vegetable garden at the far end of the courtyard. While Horonzik was digging up the ground and dividing it into flower beds with narrow paths between them, Leibel, in his shirt and vest, with a black velvet scullcap on head, followed the janitor, sowing the vegetable and flower seeds. Behind the low wooden fence of the garden, the children of the courtyard looked on curiously, some of them trying to be helpful by carrying cans of water from the pump to water the garden beds. Around the holiday of Shavuoth, a month and a half after Passover, the garden was already blooming with all kind of vegetation. The green cups of poppy were full of seeds, the round, golden sunflower disks were ablaze on tall, green stems, as the cucumbers, radishes and tomatoes ripened on the ground. The garden was now alive with butterflies and bees and was the pride of the whole courtyard.

After Shavuoth, when many children were free from the Polish school, Itzush, the landlord's nephew from Warsaw, appeared and begun to rule over the children in the yard. Itzush was a boy of about eleven, well built and nimble, with a clear, tanned face and sharp, penetrating eyes. Because he was a Warsowian and the landlord's nephew, he felt superior to the provincials around him. The children of the courtyard stuck to him and were ready to obey his commands. In the morning, when they came out into the yard, Itzush arranged them into single or double rows and began the drill.

"Attention! Trot around the yard! Stop!"

As the kids had warmed up, they began to play more exciting games of hide-and-seek, cops and robbers, and firemen. In an instant, upon Itzushe's command, the boys turned their caps backwards and became firemen. On 'fire' were the sheds along the fence of the neighbouring lumber yard. The boys began to howl like fire sirens and then attacked the locked sheds with sticks and stones. Some of them carried pails of water from the nearby pump and poured them on the dark, wooden walls of the sheds; others negotiated the low tar-papered roofs, wildly calling for more water to put out the fire. Meanwhile, the area around the pump became flooded and some annoyed adults intervened and stopped the commotion. In general, there was an ongoing war between the children and the grown-ups over the dominion of the courtyard. The children's number one enemy was, naturally, Itchele Einfeld, the landlord with the huge pot-belly and long beard. When Itchele noticed one of the boys on the roof of a shed, he became infuriated. With the pointing finger of his thick, hairy hand, he threatened the little offender and roared:

"Down, you good-for-nothing! Down, you Bolshevik! I'll teach you how to climb on roofs!"

Another antagonist of the children was Faivel the Shoemaker, who loved to raise all kind of fowl in the courtyard. Usually, the children enjoyed the presence of the winged creatures and did not harm them. However, it sometimes happened that one of the boys felt an urge to chase after a chicken or goose, which panicked and flew over the fence into the lumberyard where it got lost into the piles of beams and boards. At dusk, when Faivel let his fowl into the shed, he noticed the loss and began a prolonged investigation to find the culprit.

A protracted battle continued all during summer between Elie Shames and his son, little Simchale, who had no wish to attend Heder on such sunny days when other kids were free to roam the yard. Outraged, Elie chased his son with a leather strap to teach him obedience to his parents and the Rebbe. "You'll grow up a sheygetz, a peasant-boy! I'll chop you to pieces! Either a mentch or a corpse!" he called after him in his Warsaw Yiddish dialect.

Simchale ran away and hid himself in nooks and corners until Elie caught him and carried him off to Heder. However, an hour later, Simchale was back in the yard and the chase began anew. Elie Shames was a tall, handsome man with a clean-shorn beard and gentle features. Looking at him, it was hard to tell that he was so impoverished. One had to enter his tiny one-room apartment at the left-wing entrance of the building, to realize what a pauper he was.

Along the wall of the room were the two dishevelled beds; beside the window was a worn-out table with several creaking taborets, and beside the door—an old trunk for linen and clothes. As much as Elie tried to earn his meager livelihood—from all kinds of business or brokerage—he seldom succeeded. During the summer, Haye-Soreh, his wife, helped him out, carrying baskets of fruit and vegetables to the madams in the villas in the upper part of the city. In addition, Elie and Haye-Soreh had to bear the pain caused by their children—the wild, uncontrollable Simchale and the older daughter Rochel, as well. Rochel turned out quite an able and good looking girl, a good student at school and handy in sewing and knitting. If she were raised in a decent home, neighbours used to say, she would grow up and find a respectable husband. But she was the daughter of Elie the pauper and could not make peace with it; she was ashamed of her poverty as of an ugly sickness. Rochel's best friend was Fela, the daughter of Hershel, the well-to-do haberdashery storekeeper. Fela lived next door to Rochel, but what a difference was between their homes. Fela's place was spacious, its floor waxed in a shiny red colour, the beds covered with bedspreads and embroidered cushions, and the whole atmosphere there was satiated with contentment and relaxation.

It happened, when Rochel asked for something from her parents—a new dress, a pair of shoes, or some change to go to the movies—and she didn't get it, she went into a fit of hysteria that stirred the entire courtyard. Like a wounded animal she ran to the centre of the yard, threw herself on the ground, writhing in the dust and beating her fists over the head. Haye-Soreh, bent over Rochel, tried to raise her from the ground and, herself sobbing, implored her daughter: "Wild Tzilke, why do you mortify me? Why do you shame me in front of all?"

But mother's words and tears made Rochel even more excited. She jumped up and began to run with spread out arms towards the gate, screaming:

"To the railway tracks! I'll throw myself under the train!"

Children and adults alike ran after her, shut the gate, and called for Rivkale, Fela's mother, and Fela herself, to quieten Rochel down and lead her back into the house.

In addition to its steady dwellers, the courtyard was visited by rag collectors, wandering singers and circus performers. Each year a tall, lonely singer with an elongated stony face appeared and repeated his woeful chant:

> In the cemetery, beside a stone,
> I come to cry, all alone.
> I embrace with my bare hands
> My dear mother's monument.

O stone, stone, hard and cold,
You are dearest in all the world.

Nohum had tears in his eyes when he heard this song. Timidly, he pushed himself towards the singer and threw in his open cap the few paper-wrapped groschen Mother gave him.

"Health upon your head, yingele," the singer thanked him.

After the singer, the blind accordion player appeared. He was led by a girl dressed in a boy's outfit, with short-cut hair and a grey bag over her tiny shoulders. When the two arrived, the girl opened a small folding stool on which the accordion player sat down. After trying out for a while his instrument, the blind man began with a brief introduction: "Ladies and gentlemen, you will hear a song I composed about a tragic event that happened not long ago in Warsaw. A whole Jewish family went up in flames; eight souls charred beside each other. Listen to this sad story and be generous to a blind man and his child." Then he began his song, accompanied by the accordion:

In Warsaw on Krochmalna Street
This event happened, it's true—
Eight lives, a whole family,
In flames engulfed, in woe.

A father, a mother, six children,
The youngest on mother's lap;
Not one rescued, no one escaped,
All charred in the firetrap.

When he finished, the girl walked around with a wooden platter into which people threw five and ten groschen coins. Some even bought, for a quarter, the printed sheet with the song to be able later on to learn and sing the ballad.

It happened that the children got fed up with the noise and clamour of the yard and looked for a quiet, intimate place to rest. That place was the large attic that stretched over the entire building. One by one they went up the stairway to the upper floor and climbed the ladder leading into the attic.

Inside was dark and spooky, with only narrow strips of light penetrating here and there through the chinks of the roof. The floor, spread with tree needles, was soft and one could walk on it as on a carpet. Simchale climbed the small ladder to the opening on the roof from where he could see the houses, streets and courtyards spread out beneath. Excited, he began to crow like a rooster and recite a doggerel:

> Ku-Ku ri-Kir,
> Mother is not here.
> Where did she go?
> Nobody knows.
> What will she bring?
> A bird that sings.
> A gift for who?
> Me and you.

Afraid that Leibel will find them, Itzush hushed him and commanded:

"Down urchin! Leibel will kill us!"

"Who is afraid of Leibel?" Simchale bragged while obeying the leader's order.

Now they lay down on the soft floor and began to tell and retell stories of witches, goblins and ghosts that invade the synagogue or the ritual bath at midnight. After they rested for a while, the children began to explore the attic, discovering all kind of items that were brought over there for storage over the years. Suddenly, steps were heard from the other end of the attic. Groping in the semi-darkness, Leibel was slowly approaching and, noticing the boys, began to scream:

"Down, you time-wasters! You louts! Down!"

The children panicked and began to run towards the opening where the ladder to the staircase stood. Chasing after them, Leibel noticed Itzush and threatened him:

"Wait, wait, you sinner! You'll get your portion from the uncle!"

Downstairs, at the entrance to the staircase, Horonzik waited for the boys with his long broom. But of him the children had little fear; he was old and could hardly move on his feet. With one jump, they passed him by and ran for the safety and freedom of the courtyard.

Chapter 6
IN HEDER

Nohum was barely five years old when his father brought him to Tzalke the teacher's Heder. Tzalke's place was tucked away behind a wooden fence on the corner of two side streets. Inside the large airy room, a dozen or more children sat around a wooden table with Tzalke at the head, looking over the children and smiling benignly. On the table, beside Tzalke's open prayer book, lay a leather whip with a fur-covered handle, to remind the little ones that, although Tzalke was not strict as other teachers, they would have to obey him.

The pupils in the Heder were divided into two groups: beginners, and those who had already learned to read the Siddur. When Tzalke began to teach the little ones, the older boys used to sneak out of the room. Stealthily, they moved towards the anteroom and from there—into the yard. Tzalke overlooked all this; he was busy with the beginners and did not mind that the others enjoyed the fresh air for a while.

Outside, the kids were yet careful: the window of the Heder was open and, if they were noisy, the Rebbe might recall them. Bending down, or creeping on all fours, they passed under the window and entered the enclosed area between the house-wall and the fence. There the boys were free to prance, jostle, dig sand-tunnels or stretch out in the clear warm sand, squint their eyes, and see how the sun-rays unravelled into thin threads of light that blended and gleamed in all colours.

However, the children's leisure didn't last too long. Soon Tzalke appeared at the threshold of the anteroom and called, "Inside, brats! Inside!" The boys jumped up and, like fluttered birds returning into their nest, ran into the Heder. Then the Rebbe let out the small fry to play while the older ones, seated around the table, began to recite aloud:

> Happy are they who dwell
> In Thy house forever.
> They shall praise Thee, O Lord,
> Almighty and Eternal.

Late in the afternoon when the sun began to set, Tzalke's wife started to prepare the evening meal on the kitchen stove in the corner of the room. Smelling the homey aroma, the children became inpatient, eager to return to their homes for supper. Soon Tzalke called out, "Home, striplings!", and all of them jumped up and in a few seconds were outside, on the way home.

Two years Nohum spent at Tzalke's Heder where he mastered fluent Hebrew reading and became familiar with many passages from the Five Books. Soon there was no more that Tzalke could teach him; he needed a much advanced Rebbe. Thus, after Passover, Moshe-Avrohom took him to Yankel of Minsk where well-to-do children studied the weekly portions of the Five Books with Rashi commentary as well as the beginnings of Talmud.

Yankel of Minsk was a stout, broad-shouldered man with an ascetic face and a dark grey beard that reached to his waist. The Heder was in a small room with tiny window panes which looked out on a large neglected courtyard. Nohum longed for the bright room and sun-flooded yard at Tzalke's Heder, where the children could often play. At Yankel of Minsk's place, no time was wasted on such things. Here all were immersed in study under Yankel's tutelage or on their own, in small groups.

At noon, there was a brief recess; some students ran home for lunch, others had their repast at Heder. One day, Nohum skulked out quietly of the room and came home crying, "I don't like the new Heder! I'm afraid of the Rebbe!" Itte tried to put him at ease, but Moshe-Avrohom declared tersely, "A Jewish boy has to attend Heder! There's nothing to fear from the Rebbe." And right away, he took Nohum in his arms and carried him back to Yankel's place.

It did not take long before Nohum got used to his new teacher and even began to like him. In addition to being pious and seemingly strict, Yankel of Minsk possessed a genuine love for all the living, especially children, that awoke feelings of warmth, mixed with fear and respect, in his pupils.

All day long the children were engrossed in the study of Torah or tractates from the Mishnah and Gemara. Late afternoon the usual study-sessions ceased and the Rebbe began to delve into Midrashic lore and legend, or ethical stories and fables.

In a low, restrained voice, he told the children that often the wicked succeed in this world only to lose eternal life. God, blessed be He, created every person in His image and enhanced him with a free will to follow the righteous or wicked path. God's essence, the Shehinah, pleads with every sinner to return to the right way, because He's full of mercy and loving-kindness and wants everybody's good.

Sometimes the teacher began to describe the ordeals of the souls of the wicked in afterlife, how they were tossed from one end of the world to the other with no respite. Often such a sinner's soul is destined to transmigrate and languish back on earth to atone for its former transgressions.

Most exciting were Yankel's stories of the messianic days that were nearing, speedily in our time. Indeed, as foretold, the great war between Gog and Magog happened; millions of people were slaughtered, whole congregations perished; isn't it now the time for the Messiah to appear? The Rebbe's eyes were alight with joy when he told of the great amazement of the gentiles, seeing how the Messiah favoured the downtrodden Children of Israel, who are gathering from all corners of the world to their own land. Who can imagine the great marvels of those days, when the dead will arise from their graves and the whole world will be filled with God's radiance as the waters fill the sea.

After those intimate revival talks, Yankel used to leave the children with his wife and go over to the synagogue across the street for the evening prayer. Under the spell of the Rebbe's words, the children remained quiet for a while or continued with overheard stories about holy miracle-workers who expelled evil spirits, or the mischievous antics of the dead at midnight in the city's ritual bath or synagogue. Soon one of them got fed up with the morbid stories and proposed in the Heder-pupils lingo:

Shildren	—	Children
Shets	—	let's
Shay	—	play
Shil	—	till
Shebe	—	the Rebbe
Shomes	—	comes

In a moment the boys forgot the other-worldly stories and began their lively games. Soon the Rebbe returned and, after reciting the evening prayer, all were allowed to go home.

On the way home, Nohum often liked to enter the town's synagogue, the Bes-Medresh across the Heder. In summertime, one could hear through the open windows the hum of the praying or the voices of those studying. Inside, Nohum used to walk around the heavy wooden tables, examining some large Talmud volumes or listening to the disputes of the lads and elderly students. In a corner around a table, a group of artisans and merchants listened attentively to a discourse in talmudic lore given by a learned member of the community. Between the two stoves at the entrance to the women's gallery sat some beggars from out-of-town.

It was getting late and Nohum was ready to leave one time when, suddenly, Pinhas the Sexton arouse on the almemor in the middle of the synagogue to announce that right after the evening prayer, a Maggid would deliver a sermon. Beside Pinhas stood the Maggid, a tall, lean man with a pitch black beard and earlocks. Nohum loved to listen to the discourses of the Maggidim who visited the city from time to time. Although he did not fully grasp the meaning of their exhortations, their words filled him with a sweet sadness and longing. In this manner, Nohum thought, the ancient prophets of Israel must have wandered over the towns and hamlets of Judea to reproach and chastise the people for serving Baal and other idols.

Right after prayers, the congregation moved closer around the almemor to listen to the Maggid's discourse. At the table on the almemor, the Maggid stood silently, waiting for the commotion to end. Then he began to shake back and forth, reciting in a doleful voice:

"Our sages of blessed memory said, 'Due to three things the children of Israel were redeemed from Egypt: because they did not change their names, nor their attire and continued to observe the Sabbath.' Today, woe to us, what do we see? First of all one gets rid of his Jewish dress, further he adopts a gentile name and abandons the Yiddish tongue. Now the way is open to desecrate the Sabbath and to deny the basics of our religion.

"This is the road so many of our young people are taking—to sink deeper and deeper in the morass of impurity and lawlessness. And all this began only with a small, seemingly innocent step—throwing off the Jewish caftan and putting on a short jacket and hat. As a tree whose bark is peeled off, so a Jew

26

without his traditional garments stands bare and empty, unable to bloom or bear fruit. His Jewishness is slowly dried out and cannot be transmitted to the forthcoming generations."

The Maggid stopped for a moment to catch his breath and continued: "Gevald! Woe to us! The walls of the Bes-Medresh mourn for the thousands of Jewish children who abandoned them. And where-to did they go? Into playhouses and dance halls, into workers' locals where even the holiest of days, the Day of Atonement, is desecrated! Free men they declare themselves! Free from the yoke of the commandments, free to revel around the golden calf, as the generation of the desert did, not fearing the punishments and plagues they'll bring upon themselves and all of us."

Afterwards, the Maggid continued with fault-findings even of the observant, who obey the mitzvoth mechanically, without heart and feeling. Seldom one pities his unfortunate neighbour, or invites a poor man to share his meal. When one is better off, his window-pane becomes covered with a silvery film; it becomes a mirror in which he sees only himself. Finally, the Maggid concluded with a call for repentance and spiritual renewal which would awake God's mercy and hasten the redemption as it was foretold, "A redeemer will come to Zion, speedily in our days. Amen!"

As soon as the Maggid concluded, his prophetic fire was gone; he now became a poor homeless Jew, standing at the synagogue door to receive the charity coins people left in his outspread kerchief.

Outside, the Merchant Street was full of people; young men in white shirts with rolled up sleeves, girls in short-sleeved summer dresses—all walking and talking leisurely. In the crossroad corner, in front of Popover's restaurant, which was always full of noise and cigarette-smoke, young bareheaded men were engaged in heated discussions. Football players from the different sport clubs and their fans were arguing over the results of the latest match and elaborated on the performance of their favourite players.

Passing through the crowd, Nohum thought about the Maggid and his call for repentance. How come, Nohum wondered, that so many Jews disregard his warnings and fear not at all God's wrath and retribution?

Chapter 7
IN THE RABBI'S COURTYARD

For several seasons Nohum continued to study in the Heder of Yankel Minsker. The longer Nohum stayed there, the more he became attached to and inspired by the old teacher. Yankel too appreciated Nohum's eagerness to study the Holy Writ and its commentaries. Under the teacher's guidance, Nohum became pious and observant; he never forgot to recite the 'Shema' before bedtime or the 'Modeh Ani' as soon as he arose. He let his earlocks grow longer and asked his father to order him a black Jewish cap and a dark gaberdine, as it was customary with Hasidic children. Itte was glad to see her son in this new attire and imagined how her late father, himself a religious teacher, would have been proud of his grandson. But Moshe-Avrohom was skeptical and remarked: "I wish he would continue this way later on, when he grows up..."

When Leibel, the landlord's adopted son, saw Nohum dressed in his Hasidic garb, he pinched him lovingly on the cheek and exclaimed:

"Thus, Nohumel, thus a Jew should be adorned!"

He then proceeded to inquire about the weekly Torah portion and what does Rashi say on the verse, "But the children struggled in her womb." Without hesitation, Nohum poured out, in traditional intonation, the proper midrashic answer:

"When Rivka, the wife of Isaac, was passing by the House of Study of Shem and Eber, Jacob struggled to come out; when she approached a place of idol worship, Esau grappled to get out..."

"Health upon your head, my child!" Leibel rejoiced. "May God bless you and watch over you, that you continue on the right path."

"Amen!" answered Nohum piously.

Soon after the holiday of Shavuoth, Yankel of Minsk fell ill and could not go on teaching. His face turned yellowish, his eyes became dull and caved in, and he moaned quietly, in pain. The Rebbe's wife busied herself around her husband, handing him a glass of boiled water whitened with a bit of milk or a small bowl of cooked cereal. Quietly, as not to disturb her sick man, she muttered complaints and reproaches against her son Velvel who, together with his older brother, Meirel, brought their father to such a pitiful state.

It was no secret in town that both sons of the venerated teacher got "spoiled" and abandoned the pious ways of their father. Instead of spending his time in the nearby House of Study, or elsewhere in a Yeshivah, Velvel preferred the free life of the bazaar. There he walked around with a large wooden tray strung to his shoulders, selling all kinds of pastry which his sister, Brayna, baked at home in the small back room adjoining the Heder. Because he still lodged at his parents' home, Velvel continued to wear his Jewish garb and avoided to break the laws of the Sabbath in public. However, Meirel, his brother, left years ago father's home, learned to be a house painter and became a leader among the "Workers of Zion", a secular, left-wing Zionist organization. Thus Yankel of Minsk could not pride himself with both his sons and the deep grievance that nurtured him surely did not add to his well-being.

For a few days during the rebbe's sickness, Velvel continued to teach his father's pupils. Afterwards, as the Rebbe's condition worsened, the children were sent to their homes.

The next morning, everybody around knew that Yankel of Minsk had passed away. Nohum and a few other pupils gathered in the courtyard, in front of the teacher's house. Inside, both Velvel and Meirel, together with a few other men, recited from the Book of Psalms; candles were lit on the floor at the head of the covered corpse, and the small mirror on the wall was wrapped in a dark cloth. From the adjoining room the sobbings of Yankel's wife and daughter could be heard.

After midday, the hearse with Yankel's coffin was driven into the street beside the entrance to the House of Study. Inside, the place was full of people who came to depart from the beloved teacher and to listen to the eulogy of the city's old Rabbi. Soon the funeral procession began to move towards Karczew Street, to the town's Eternal Place.

A few days after the demise of Yankel, Moshe-Avrohom led Nohum to the Heder of the Baranower. The teacher from Baranow was not one of the most reputable in town; he was known for his bad temper and for not sparing the rod on his pupils. Because of this, the Heder boys made up the following limerick:

29

The Baranower is a brute;
When he is in a bad mood
He'll butcher and slay --
Oy-vey! Oy-vey!

The Baranower was a tall Jew with an overgrown beard and earlocks from which his dark eyes and long red nose stared out. People whispered that he probably became a melamed out of need, having no other means of earning a livelihood. Thus he was destined to a life of strife and struggle with his pupils with whom he had no rapport.

When enraged by the mischief of the boys, he grabbed one of them, laid him on his knees, pulled down his pants, and began to trash his ass with his old, frayed leather strap. The kids, strong and healthy sons of butchers or ritual slaughterers, got used to these trashings and continued to devote their whole energy to make the life of the Rebbe miserable. Thus they worked up all kind of stratagems and tricks, like hiding the Rebbe's strap when he took a nap, or sending out a paper aeroplane in the midst of reciting a passage from the Torah, and similar mischief.

Annoyed and irritated, the Baranower raised his eyes to the ceiling, as if calling for Heaven's help, muttering to himself, "Master of the Universe! I can't go on any more!" Soon his helplessness turned into rage; he began to run after the troublemakers, shouting: "I'll mortify you! I'll tear you to pieces!" The boys ran, jumped over the benches, hid themselves in the corners or under the table, yelling and screaming, "Not me, Rebbe! Not me!" Finally the Baranower grabbed one of them, laid him over his knees, and began the trashing ritual until his anger subsided.

The Baranower's Heder was in a large, gloomy room on the second floor of an old building in the courtyard of the Hasidic Rabbi of Otwock. The ceiling of the room consisted of heavy wooden beams and the walls were plastered with whitewash as in peasants' cottages. The place was neglected; spider's web hung in the corners of the ceiling and layers of dust were on the closets with large, leather-bound religious books. The Rebbe's wife, a tall haggard woman, walked around in silence, not daring to interfere into her husband's business.

From time to time the children got a recess and were let out into the large courtyard. In the center of the yard was a huddle of wooden houses, leaning one on the other. To the right was the Otwock Rabbi's synagogue, empty during weekdays but alive on Saturdays and holidays. Beside the House of Prayer was the Rabbi's living quarters and further on—dwellings for his close ones, relatives, poor scholars, and others.

On Saturdays and the holidays the Rabbi's prayer-house was filled with his followers and admirers. The hanging lamps were lit, candles burned, and the hum of prayer and song was all over the place. The fenced area behind the synagogue was full of Hasidim in black silken gaberdines, some wearing edged fur hats, all wrapped in woolen prayer-shawls, strolling back and forth, engaged in discussion of Torah-matters or politics of the different Hasidic dynasties.

During fall and winter, the courtyard was empty, its trees barren, and the grassy ground covered in mud or snow. However, in mid-December, during the holiday of Hanukkah, the Rabbi's place became enlivened anew. Each night of the eight-day holiday, the Heder children of the area, especially those from the nearby community school—the Talmud Torah—gathered to witness the ceremony of lighting the Hanukkah candles. The children were standing on the heavy wooden tables and benches from where they could view the beadle lighting the large Hanukkah candelabra. As soon as he appeared, they burst out in a loud rhythmic chant, "He walks! He walks! He walks!" The sexton approached one of the windows and began inserting the coloured candles into the menorah, while the children kept on reciting: "He loads! He loads! He loads!"

As soon as the shames lit the candles and placed the menorah on the window sill, the children roared anew: "He lights! He lights! He lights!"

Happy and excited they soon left the House of Study, hurrying over the snow-covered streets to their homes for parties with fried potato patties and dreidel games.

Even more memorable was later on, in mid-winter, the holiday of Purim. The preparations for the holiday began several weeks before and involved young and old. The Heder boys prepared their masks and costumes; the housewives were busy baking the sweet three-cornered Hamantaschen, while the members of the

Bikkur Holim—Visiting the Sick Society—prepared for the yearly Purim parade during which the funds for the upkeeping of the Society were collected.

The Bikkur Holim parade began the morning of Purim and continued till late in the afternoon. Nohum got up early to walk with his father to the premises of the Society in a villa at the far end of Swiderska Street. The Society's two room place was full of members who already completed the morning prayers and were tasting hurriedly snacks of herring and egg-cakes with a sip of brandy before they'll begin to change into the Purim costumes. Soon everyone was trying on old pants and jackets of Polish Hussars, Russian Cossacks, or Austro-Hungarian officers which were rented for this occasion from theater garderobes in Warsaw. Some of them put on transparent masks, others picked up drums, trumpets or an accordion to enliven the parties to which they were assigned. These were dispatched to the hotels, villas and sanatoria in the better section of the town where they were to entertain the guests and the owners alike, and collect from them the yearly donations for the Society.

Outside, in the villa in front of the Bikkur Holim premises, a crowd of curious, mostly women, young lads and children, gathered to gape and cheer the Purim players. The highlight of the event was the appearance of Yonele Sharfhartz, a milk merchant and owner of a fine horse and wagon with which he used to deliver the large milk cans to the hotels and resorts. At the Purim parade, he usually appeared on his horse, dressed in a general's uniform, with golden epaulets and a sabre at his right waist. Beside Yonele, marched on foot other prominents of the Society, all in elaborate and colourful uniforms.

One by one the parties left the grounds and began marching along Swiderska Street towards the bazaar and beyond, to villas above the railway tracks. As they passed by, doors were opened and people cheered them and admired their outlandish costumes and masks. Here and there, on the way, the Purim players entered a store of one of the better-off merchants and began to dance and play noisily until they were sent away with a satisfactory contribution. In some places, the players were received with wine and cake or a thimbleful of whiskey; the Purim paraders cheered, with the traditional "to life," wished the patrons a good year and bargained for a higher donation, reminding the merchants that it is for the sake of the poor and sick of their brethren. Cheered up, the Bikkur Holim players continued to other places of the city.

All the day of Purim Nohum was outside, trying to be everywhere and see everything. First he lingered at the Bikkur Holim place to see his father dressed up and leaving with his group. However, Moshe-Avrohom was not in a hurry; he let others pick out the costumes they liked and put on whatever was left himself. Nohum resented that his father was not dressed up in a fine outfit, like the others. Even on Purim, Moshe-Avrohom seemed to be serious and reserved, and did not let himself go like the rest of the people. It didn't take long and Nohum would lose sight of his father's group. But other Purim players were in abundance all around. Heder children in colourful paper masks and crowns appeared in small groups before the doors of the inhabitants to receive their Purim money or treats. Here and there Nohum recognized among them some of his friends from Heder or the street. Chilled and exhausted, he would return home late in the afternoon to wait for his father's arrival and the traditional Purim meal that followed it.

After the Purim upheaval, the town would return to its usual wintery stagnation. However, people were comforted by the first omens of the approaching spring which reminded them that Passover, the holiday of freedom and renewal, was only a few weeks away.

Chapter 8
THE RESTAURANT

For some time Moshe-Avrohom walked around disquieted and worried: there was little work in the shop and the apprentices had to be paid and the family fed and provided for. In addition, promissory notes kept on arriving, while the cobblers did not pay their debts. Times were hard and many small businessmen defaulted. Uneasy about his affairs, Moshe-Avrohom often left the shop to find a short-term loan and thus be able to continue for a while. Back in the shop, he sat down to busy himself with his accounts, thinking aloud: "Can't go on...We'll have to try something else..." For Nohum and the other children, he had no patience and he squabbled with his wife continuously.

"I told you! I warned you," argued Itte plaintively. "You loaned away everything to those thievish cobblers, may they lie sick forever!"

"Quit it, woman!" Moshe-Avrohom pleaded impatiently.

"Such a softie!" Itte continued. "A nice Jew—only for others, not for his wife and kids."

"Quiet!" shouted Moshe-Avrohom and jumped up to his feet as if scalded.

"I won't be quiet! I'll scream in the streets!" Itte retorted.

Enraged, Moshe-Avrohom grabbed a bootleg and began to trash his wife over her head and body. Seeing that Father was beating up Mom, the children began to sob and scream, and Shaindel ran over to pull him away. "Father dear, don't hit her!" she cried.

Moshe-Avrohom let up his wife and rushed out of the shop.

For a few days he walked around quiet and reticent. Also Itte and the children trudged around the house in silence. A sadness hung in the back room and over the shop that suddenly became empty and muted. The two apprentices were sent away because Moshe-Avrohom decided to close shop and open a restaurant in its place. The city grew constantly and was full of newcomers and guests—Moshe-Avrohom thought. The few restaurants in the area, around the bazaar, were all doing well and there is surely place for another one—he decided.

34

Soon carpenters showed up and began to transform the boot-stitching shop into a restaurant. They tore down the wall shelves, built up the buffet and the shop window, and brought in new tables and chairs.

In the back room, Itte and Shaindel tied up the bedding and other house belongings, which were loaded, together with the heads of the two sewing machines, into a horse-drawn wagon and moved to a rented room on the nearby Merchant Street, at Shiele Klapetsky's place.

Shiele, the patriarch of a branched out family of cobblers and shoe merchants, was a dried out old man with a frayed little beard, always jolly and nimble. With his sons and daughters on their own, Shiele remained alone with his wife, Broche, and he was now more concerned with the world to come than with this transitory place of the living. After a few hours of work at his cobbler's table, he walked over to the nearby House of Study to participate in a learning session or in plain talk of fellow Jews. He was also active in the society, "Supporters of the Poor", which organized a food bank for impoverished and needy families. Saturday noon, right after the service in the synagogue, he used to walk the streets and courtyards of the area with another fellow and collect the food in a large straw basket.

It was here, in Shiele and Broche's back room, that Moshe-Avrohom and his family moved in after opening the restaurant. The room was quite large, but dark and eerie; its low window faced a small, fenced yard where dilapidated wooden stairs led to an upper apartment occupied by Shiele's son-in-law, also a shoemaker and seller of second-rate footwear on weekly market days.

Hurriedly, Moshe-Avrohom reassembled the closet and the beds, squeezed in the sewing machines in a corner and went, together with his wife, to attend the newly opened restaurant. The children were left on their own and had to walk each morning to the restaurant where Itte prepared their breakfast and sent off the girls to school and Nohum to Heder.

Along the wall in the restaurant there stood the glass-covered buffet with fresh bread and pastries and a variety of appetizers from Itte's kitchen: platters with slices of herring dipped in oil and adorned with plasters of onion, hard-boiled eggs, fried liver portions and roasted cuts of goose or breast-meat, beside dried and moist rolls of salami. In the wall cabinet behind the buffet were bottles and flasks of lemonade and packs of cigarettes. In the store-window, empty bottles of beer and wine were displayed beside baskets with egg-cookies and cuts of strudel and cake. Over the window and on the doors, tin signboards showing foaming glasses of golden-yellow beer were attached.

Beside the buffet stood the shiny beer machine for regular and black-sweet beer. Sweating and wobbling, Moshe-Avrohom carried on his back the heavy beer barrels from the beer yard near the market. After inserting them into the machine, he donned a waiter's jacket and proceeded to attend the customers. In this, he was helped by Shaindel who had to give up her studies in the Polish school to help out in the business. Meanwhile, Itte was busy all day in the kitchen, behind a wooden separation in the back room, where she prepared the food and dishes for the patrons and her own household.

In mid-summer, both rooms of the restaurant were full of diners and guests from the city and out-of-town. Merchants and suppliers of grain and fruit, eggs and poultry, arrived from the towns and villages near Lublin to provide for the pensions, dachas and sanatoria. The goods were unloaded at the railway ramp by the porters and delivered on horse-driven carts to their destination. The porters and draymen were hulky Jews with overgrown beards, dressed in worn-out cotton jackets. Their sons, who continued in the same trade, were hardy, broad-shouldered men with shaved red faces and untrimmed hair. Playfully they loaded the heavy sacks of grain or wooden crates with fruit into the carts at the ramp, laughing and jostling each other on the way.

Around the out-of-town merchants gathered a host of brokers and middlemen who tried to earn a few zlotys from the provincial suppliers. After the produce was unloaded, all of them—merchants, porters, draymen and brokers—hurried into the restaurants and beer halls to complete deals and settle accounts at tables with glasses of beer and a quick meal. The porters and draymen raved, yelled obscenities or tapped good-naturedly the merchants' shoulders, trying to squeeze out from them a few more zlotys for their sweat and toil. The merchants, tough village and small-town Jews, swore by their wives and kids that they could not add a groschen, otherwise they would lose money from their own pockets.

From time to time noisy squabbles and altercations broke out among them; tongues got loose from the alcoholic beverages; soon fists went into motion and bodies became entangled in bitter strifes. Scared to death, Itte ran into the street wringing her hands and screaming: "Woe is me! They'll kill each other! They'll overturn the place! Such a bitter livelihood!"

Usually, when such a fracas broke out, the "tough guys" appeared and restored order. Their chief was Duvtchele the son of Leib-Itzel, a guy with a pock-marked face and a pair of muscular arms that were created, so it seems, for fights and brawls.

About Duvtchele's daring deeds many stories were told in town. More than once he participated in feuds and encounters with knives and iron gloves, and the devil did not get him—he came out with only a few scars here and there. Duvtchele was feared even by the strong guys among the porters and butchers; he was supple and daring like a tiger, wanton and undaunted by anything. Besides, Duvtchele had behind him an iron wall —his father Leib-Itzel the draymen and his three brothers, Meir, Done, and Joel. Meir and Done were baggage porters at the train station; Joel was a coachman on a droshky. Although he was the youngest and the smallest of his brothers and limped on his right foot, one could well count on him when it came to defend his clan. People used to say that he, little Joel, was the most dangerous of the brothers; it was indeed a miracle that he became crippled in his youth, otherwise he would overturn the town.

As soon as the "tough guys" arrived, the quarreling parties were separated and forced to hold a "Torah court." One of them served as "Judge"; he listened to the arguments of both parties and pronounced the verdict which all had to obey. Meanwhile, the litigants had to provide beer and refreshments for all the company.

At the end of summer, when the provincial merchants returned to their homes, business in Moshe-Avrohom's restaurant slowed down. To acquire a steady clientele for the fall and winter, Itte began to cook a hot barley soup for the street vendors, newspaper carriers, and others that happened to come in for a repast.

Among the steady customers of this inexpensive meal was the "professor," an elderly gentleman with a bald pate and missing teeth. He was a private tutor, always engrossed in reading books and magazines in foreign languages. In spite of his erudition, he was often moneyless and had to get his meal on credit. Itte pitied him and used to add a bit more barley and meat to his plate.

"What's the use of being learned, when you don't make a decent living?" she argued.

"Better to be impoverished than be like these gross beings," answered the "professor," pointing to street-lads at the other tables.

Another steady customer was Ruben the Thief. From his youth Ruben was engaged in his trade, stealing from cottages and pension-rooms jewellery and other valuables which he sold afterwards for peanuts. From time to time he was apprehended, spent long months in jail, but as soon as he was out, he returned to his old trade.

At the entrance to the restaurant often lingered a boy clothed in rags and tatters. He was called the "Gilgul," a lost or transmigrated soul. His parents, Joshke the coachman and Leah "Whack" were separated and left their son to anybody's care. Sometimes Joshke came by on his droshky and stopped for a while to hand over to his son a bagel with cheese or some small change. Soon Leah appeared and husband and wife began to abuse each other aloud until Joshke lifted his whip over his horse and departed.

"Have a good day, my tart," he called out leaving.

"Be singed, my scoundrel!" Leah responded in a high pitch.

It happened also that one of the "tough guys" pitied the "Gilgul" and bought him a roll with salami and a drink. Most of all was interested in the boy the Pole Malczyk. He was a tall man with a thick brown mustache, in style of the Polish gentry of old. Malczyk was a building contractor and, after a long summer-day's work, he loved to sit for hours in the restaurant over a mug of beer and chat with whomever he could. Malczyk was well versed in the Old Testament and spoke with reverence of the Jews, the covenant-people from whom the Lord Jesus descended. He commiserated the "Gilgul," took him from time to time to the barber for a haircut and often bought him something to eat.

Nohum loved to sit in the restaurant and observe the porters, draymen and other street-lads that congregated there. How different were they from the bent, worn out Jews in town. They were lively and talkative, strong and broad-shouldered and had neither fear for gentiles nor for the authorities. They lived carefree lives, relished in eating and drinking as long as there was money in the pocket and often shared their food with comrades and even strangers. And should a Polish hooligan start with a Jew on the market or elsewhere, they would not be afraid to go after him and teach a lesson with a few "dry" blows here and there.

Bent over a table in a corner of the restaurant, Nohum listened eagerly to their boastful tales of encounters with Jewish or Polish maid-servants. Some of them had "brides"—mistresses in the nearby town of Falenice or in the Warsaw suburb of Praga. On the weekends they used to leave their wives and children and visit their paramours and sweethearts. Back home, they told each other of their adventures and romantic exploits. Moshe-Avrohom was quite unhappy with Nohum staying so often in the restaurant. "The boy is being ruined here," he complained to his wife. "He learns of too much depravity from these guys."

"Don't say this," Itte disagreed. "Our Nohumel is a pure soul. No dirt will stick to him."

Chapter 9
ON HACHSHARAH

During the summer season, Moshe-Avrohom and his wife had to labour in the restaurant from dawn to midnight every day, including Sabbath and holidays. Although he was not strictly observant—he wore a short jacket and did shave his beard—yet it pained him to be forced to work on the Sabbath.

On Friday, late in the afternoon, the front door and shutters of the restaurant were closed and Moshe-Avrohom with his family were ready to celebrate the day of rest in the back room of the restaurant. Here, in the middle of the room, two restaurant tables were joined and covered with a white tablecloth. Itte lit the Sabbath candles and whispered the blessing, while her hands covered her face. After returning from the synagogue, Moshe-Avrohom recited aloud the Sanctification over a cup of wine, and the whole family sat down for the Friday night meal.

Saturday morning, Moshe-Avrohom attended the prayer service at the Visiting the Sick Society, where he was a long-standing member. Upon return from prayers, the family's Saturday noon meal was held again in the restaurant back room.

Instead of taking a Sabbath afternoon nap, as most Jews of the older generation did, Moshe-Avrohom had then to attend his patrons who had begun entering the restaurant by the back door, in the courtyard. Summer afternoon, after a full Sabbath meal, many were eager to have a mug of cold beer, and Moshe-Avrohom could not deny them this—because of the Sabbath—while the other restaurateurs in the area let their patrons in through half-closed front or side doors.

At first Moshe-Avrohom tried to work out some credit system of cards with the names of his patrons and with different folding price tags and thus avoid the handling of cash on the holy day. However, he realized that this would not do; he'd lose track of the given out credit. He also remembered how his boot shop came to ruin because of his gullibility towards his patrons. There was no choice but to accept payment and attend the customers even on the Sabbath day.

Dressed in their best, with uncovered heads and freshly shaved faces, the porters and draymen came, some with their wives or girlfriends, for a refreshing drink and a tasty appetizer. The Sabbath table was hurriedly taken apart, the brass candlesticks hidden away, and soon the room was, as usual, full of noisy chat and clamour. Moshe-Avrohom tried in vain to quieten his customers; he bit his lips and continued silently to fill the beer glasses and deliver the plates with snacks.

To accept payment from the patrons was Shaindel's task. She had, therefore, to remain in the restaurant the whole Sabbath afternoon, when girls of her age were free to saunter on the streets or spend time in the youth clubs of the various organizations. Dressed in a white embroidered blouse, she hurried from the front store to the back room, attending the customers with a friendly word or smile. However, her eyes were sad and dim and a hidden anger brewed in her. For she had to stay put even on the day of rest among these rude and noisy people whose vulgar talk made her face often burn with shame.

For some time Shaindel had been visiting the club of the Hechalutz, a youth organization of the Workers' of Zion party. Sometimes in the evening when it was quiet in the restaurant, she ran over for an hour or more to the Hechalutz club which was always full of youth. Some were singing or dancing, others simply sat and chatted or were engaged in sessions at which Jewish problems were tackled. The walls of both rooms of the club were adorned with portraits of Theodore Herzl, Ben-Gurion, and others, or maps of the Land of Israel and posters of the Jewish National Fund. On a table in the corner lay in disorder some of the movements' propaganda literature—brochures and booklets with reports of the progress of the Jewish colonization of Eretz Israel.

From there Shaindel brought home some of these books and pamphlets, which she eagerly read in her free time. Nohum was already nine years old and had taught himself to read Yiddish from the daily Yiddish paper which was around in the restaurant. Out of curiosity he began to look into Shaindel's booklets and slowly a new horizon opened before him—the Land of Israel reborn.

As any Jewish boy, Nohum was familiar with Eretz Israel from the Five Books he studied in Heder. He knew of Beth-El where Jacob saw in his dream the angels of Israel ascending and the fiery messengers of outside of Israel descending from heaven. He remembered Beer-Sheba, where Abraham and Isaac dug wells and water cisterns, or Hebron and the Double Cave, where the Patriarchs and their spouses lay buried. Only Rachel alone was buried on the road to Bethlehem because Jacob foresaw by the Holy Spirit that Nevuzradan, the Babylonian chieftain, will lead down this road the Jewish captives into Babylon. And when they'll pass by, exhausted and dejected, Rachel will rise from her grave and lament for them. Then a heavenly voice would be heard, comforting the deportees with the promise of return to their possession and inheritance. Nohum also read in the Talmud of Titus the Wicked who burned and razed the Holy Temple and scattered the Jews all over the world. Only the study of Torah and the strict observance of its numerous commandments will quicken the coming of the Messiah and bring redemption to his people.

However, according to Shaindel's brochures and books, the redemption of the Jewish people would come about in an entirely different way. Here, Nohum learned, Jews should not wait at all for the Messiah, but go on their own to the Promised Land in order to build and possess it. Thousands of young Jews and Jewesses are leaving their homes, stealing across borders and travelling over sea and land to reach Eretz Israel or Palestine, as the gentiles call it. There they plant trees and plough the ground, dry the swamps and pasture flocks, build all kinds of settlements, villages and towns, even a big city named Tel-Aviv. Often they have to defend themselves from the Arabs who try to drive out the Jews from the colonies and settlements. However, the halutzim are not intimidated; they possess guns, pistols and swords and defend themselves successfully.

Often, in long winter evenings, Nohum began to sit beside Shaindel and listen to her tales of halutzim, who leave their homes and go for Hachsharah in faraway towns in Poland, to prepare themselves for life in Eretz Israel. There the young men and women learn hard work, in the fields or factories, and the communal way of life. Thus they become halutzim, pioneers and trailblazers for others who will follow in their footsteps. After living and working on Hachsharah for several years, many of them become eligible to receive a "certificate"—a permit to emigrate to Eretz Israel. But the British, who rule Palestine, are no more friendly to the Jews and reduce from year the number of issued "certificates." The halutzim have, therefore, no choice but to enter the land illegally.

And here Shaindel lowered her voice and confided to Nohum that she, too, is thinking seriously of leaving home for Hachsharah, but is afraid of revealing it to Father and Mother. She doubts if they will allow her to realize her dream and let her go away. Mother especially will argue that she, the oldest one, is needed home to look after the children and help out in the restaurant. While Shaindel explained the matter to Nohum, tears appeared in her eyes and she began to croon pensively one of her favourite songs:

> The sun goes down in flames,
> The wide horizon gleams;
> Thus is vanishing my hope,
> Thus fades away my dream.

Suddenly, like a thunderbolt on a clear day, Moshe-Avrohom's family learned that Shaindel was going to leave home for Hachsharah. It happened at the beginning of summer when the maiden was so needed in the restaurant from which the family drew its livelihood. Moshe-Avrohom was deeply disturbed, hesitant to agree or disapprove his daughter's decision. The girl was indispensable in the household, both to care for his five younger children and as a helpmate in the restaurant. While his wife was busy most of the time preparing the meals and delicacies in the kitchen, Shaindel would attend the patrons in her loveable, friendly manner. In general, how could he allow her, at the tender age of seventeen, to leave home for some faraway place, where she'll have to do all kind of manual work and live in a commune, men and women together?

On the other hand, the matter was not at all so simple. The girl wanted so much to leave, her tearful eyes pleaded with him all the time as if saying, "Father dear, allow me to go!" Moshe-Avrohom realized that in the long run he would not be able to hold her back. Was it wise to restrain her? Isn't she going on Hachsharah to prepare herself for life in the Land of Israel? There halutzim build villages and towns and lay the foundation for a Jewish state. All this is not a mirage, a light-hearted adventure. The Yiddish newspapers are full with reports and pictures about their deeds and achievements. Who knows, maybe these daring young men and women will bring the long-awaited redemption of the Jews? In due time, we will have a land of our own and we will be able to leave Poland where, after dwelling for many centuries, Jews are still treated as strangers and second-class citizens. He will allow her to leave, Moshe-Avrohom finally decided. He'll let her go her own way, and with the help of the One Above, she'll reach the shores of the land of our forefathers.

On hearing that Shaindel was given permission to leave, Itte began to grumble: "With no luck, one is better off not to be born. In other families you have great use from a maiden her age, and here—nothing. She is going away God knows where, only not to stay at home, where she is needed."

Moshe-Avrohom remained silent, as if he didn't hear his wife's complaints. This irritated Itte even more and she continued in a pitched voice: "What kind of a father are you? To let your own child go away to the edge of the world, where she'll have to drag beams, scrub floors and eat stale bread and water together with a bunch of good-for-nothings—is this her future? Doesn't she have a home where to live and be useful?" "Enough! Enough!" Moshe-Avrohom retorted impatiently. "We heard already all this!" Itte fell silent, her eyes shining with tears.

"Let her go, Itte!" Moshe-Avrohom said softly. "You'll see, we will somehow manage without her. With God's help, she'll reach Eretz Israel and in time we, too, will follow her."

Touched by her husband's comforting words, Itte broke into deep sobbing. Big tears streamed down her careworn face and her slender body trembled as she spoke:

"Is it my fault that we have such a bitter life? To work day and night with no Sabbath or holiday. And the children, too, are left to themselves, as if they didn't have a mother, God forbid! Nu, Let her go! Let her go!" She concluded, wiping the tears with the edge of her apron.

The next Saturday night, Shaindel's comrades from the Hechalutz movement arranged a farewell party for her. The back room of the restaurant was full of young people, all of them in high spirits, talking aloud or singing Hebrew and Yiddish songs. The boys, in short-sleeved shirts, with dishevelled forelocks and uncovered heads, toasted on wine and beer glasses and praised Shaindel's courage and resolve to realize her Zionist convictions. The girls, in white blouses, hair braided or short-cut, kissed and embraced Shaindel over and over. Many brought her farewell gifts or wrote hearty inscriptions in her diary booklet. Moshe-Avrohom provided beer and snacks and the youngsters ate and drank heartily. A clownish young man climbed a chair and began to sing in a sentimental vein:

> Listen, you beautiful maiden,
> What will you do
> In that faraway Land?

"Down with him!" others yelled. "Let's sing real halutzic songs!"

> O, when, when, sings a halutz?
> When he lives in the Kibbutz.
> There his hunger is often strong,
> Instead of eating, he sings a song.

Soon the leaders of the Hechalutz Organization began their farewell orations in which they touched on the problems of the movement and the latest developments in the Land of Israel. With singing of the Hatikvah and solemn calls of "Next year in the built-up Jerusalem" the farewell party concluded.

Next day, Shaindel was ready to leave for her Hachsharah site in a remote industrial town in Upper Silesia. All morning neighbours and friends came in for the final goodbye. The women cried and showered her with kisses, blessings and good wishes. Itte cried most of all and asked her stepdaughter's forgiveness for treating her often more harshly than her own children. Shaindel walked around tired and excited from all the commotion. She packed her belongings in two large suitcases and proceeded to embrace and kiss her little brother and sisters, giving each one some going-away money.

At the railway station, a group of close friends gathered again and cheered up Shaindel with songs and words of encouragement. Moshe-Avrohom carried the suitcases into the wagon and embraced his daughter. "Go in health and return in health. And, please, write often," he said, trying to conceal his emotion.

"I shall write, dear father!" Shaindel assured him in tears.

Finally Shaindel embraced her beloved Nohum.

"Now, Nohumel, you are the oldest of the children. Try to help as much as you can. And write of everything!"

The whistling signal was heard and Shaindel entered the compartment. For a while she stood at the window, waving her last goodbyes to her dear ones. The train disappeared, carrying her into the open, wide world.

Chapter 10
BACK TO THE WORKSHOP

Since Shaindel left home, Moshe-Avrohom's household became even more neglected. The work in the restaurant was too hard for Itte. She had to rise at dawn for the farmers' market to buy the produce and then continue all day long at the hot kitchen stove behind the division in the back room of the restaurant. Standing there, she often felt a sharp pinching under her left arm and had to sit down for a while to catch her breath. At other times, she was seeing dark particles blinking before her eyes. She was scared, but did not dare to tell of her weakness to her husband or anyone else.

"I'm losing my strength. Who knows if I'll be able to endure?" Silently she prayed to the Master of the World: "Would I, at least, live to see my firstborn under the wedding canopy!"

Remembering her children, her strength seemed to well up as from a hidden reservoir. The children, long may they live, are growing up nicely. Nohumel, no Evil Eye on him, will soon become Bar-Mitzvah. And the girls, Tema and Rochel, how they grew up in no time. Tema is slender, with dark braids and dark-brown eyes, and Rochel—blond, with flaxen hair like a village girl. Also Godele, her second son, may he grow up healthy, is a precious boy, clever and sharp and willing to obey and help out. He attends already Heder and will soon have to be enrolled in the Polish School. After him she bore another girl, Malkele, with golden hair and a speckled face, still small and hardly able to walk on her tiny feet. To bear more children is not anymore for her; even this one came about accidentally.

During the week Itte had no time to care for her children. Summertime, after returning from school, they played on the street or in the courtyard. When hungry, they entered the back room of the restaurant to be fed by Mother. She provided them with whatever there was in the store: fresh kaiser rolls with swiss cheese or salami, omelettes and freshly fried hamburgers. At least, let them eat well, she thought. More than nourishment, for themselves and the children, she and Moshe-Avrohom her husband, do not get from all the work in their business. Only on

Fridays, in the afternoon, Itte found time to shampoo the children's heads and change their clothes for the Sabbath. When Shaindel was home, it was much easier for her and the children. Shaindel was neat and hardworking and you could depend on her. But she had to get this weird idea of leaving for Hachsharah. Three years passed and there was no end to it; she has not yet left for Palestine. But Itte had to keep all these thoughts to herself. Moshe-Avrohom did not allow her to utter a word against his daughter, still believing that everything will end well: Shaindel will settle in the Land of Israel, and later on they, too, will join her there. During those three years, Shaindel had visited home only twice, and for a short time only. She had changed, gained weight, and her hands were calloused from hard work in factories of Upper Silesia. The Kibbutz which she had joined when she left home fell apart; most of its members could not stand the drudgery and the spartan existence of the commune and left for their homes. The few that remained were transferred to other Hachsharah locations. But Shaindel did not even consider returning home. Without the hope of making aliyah, life for her made no sense. After staying home and enjoying family and friends for several days, she packed her suitcases and left.

From time to time a letter from her arrived, sometimes with a photograph. Shaindel's letters were long and sentimental, a blend of sadness and joy, pain and hope. The gates of Palestine were shut; one had to wait for years to receive the permit to enter the country. Meanwhile, the years of her youth passed in hard work, far away from her dear ones.

When a letter from Shaindel arrived, its reading was put off till Saturday at mealtime, when everyone was around the festive table. Nohum read aloud and all around listened attentively. From time to time a vague smile appeared on Moshe-Avrohom's face and he uttered:

"I'm sure she'll soon get her "certificate"...And then we'll think about ourselves. God willing, we may all be there in no time..."

Indeed, Moshe-Avrohom was fed up with life in Poland. "It's too much to endure," he often thought. "Anti-Semitism is growing by the day, taxes are unbearable, and there is talk about war with Germany or Russia."

Some time ago, he considered emigrating to Bizobidzhan, the Jewish Autonomous District in the Far East of Soviet Russia, on the Manchurian border. At that time, an international society was formed to promote colonization of Bizobidzhan and Jewish workingmen from the Soviet-Union and abroad willing to go there, were promised all kind of assistance. After a while, the tumult about Bizobidzhan quietened and nothing was heard of anybody from Poland going there. Palestine was, however, quite different. Despite Arab resistance and British limitations, the Yishuv was constantly growing and Jews all over were wholeheartedly behind this great endeavour.

Nohum was not only the family's reader of Shaindel's letters, he also had to respond her in everyone's name. Through this letter-exchange, Nohum learned much about his older sister and she became very dear to him. Memories of his childhood awoke, when Shaindel used to put him to bed with song and stories or when she fed and clothed him like a mother. Shaindel's life-dream of settling in the Land of Israel became dear to Nohum and he saw in his mind himself and the whole family implanted in its soil, together with millions of Jews from all over, as it is written: "Each man under his vine and fig tree."

In a nook, in Shiele Klapetsky's back room, were tucked away the heads of Moshe-Avrohom's sewing machines and other tools of his trade with which it was hard for him to part when he turned into a restaurateur. Who knows what might happen, he thought. Some day they might yet be useful in his struggle for a livelihood.

So far, Moshe-Avrohom could not complain: during the summer season, the restaurant provided him and his family quite well, and he was even able to save a few hundred zlotys for the slack fall and winter months.

Meanwhile winter had just began, the snow-filled and frozen days crept along slowly and depressingly. However, electricity bills had to be paid, various government taxes accumulated, and the children had to be provided with an education. Moshe-Avrohom worried that he'll be forced to spend the money he saved during summer, and even these will not suffice. Also, he hated to be idle. From his youth he used to work and provide for himself and his family. He, therefore, tried during those slack months to do some additional business like supplying barrels of herring or crates with sardines to the groceries in the neighbourhood, but nothing came out of all these ventures.

Moshe-Avrohom then realized that the only thing he could do to help himself during the winter was to rebuild, somehow on a smaller scale, his old boot-stitching shop. However, this was not an easy task because he had been out of the trade for years and meanwhile young artisans opened shops in the area. Still, he would be able to find work in the cheaper lines, like stitching old remade shoe tops, sandals or gaiters, for the vendors on the market or manufacturers in Warsaw. But all this could not be accomplished while he resided in Shiele Klapetsky's back room, which was too far from the restaurant and did not even have a separate entrance. To refurbish, even partially, his workshop, Moshe-Avrohom had to find a more spacious and closer living quarters.

Around Passover, a two-room apartment on the second floor of the same building as the restaurant became available and Moshe-Avrohom rented it immediately. As soon as he assembled the beds and the wooden closet in the second room, he set himself to restore his workshop in the first room. The two sewing machines were placed back-to-back beside the window and the cutting board was set high on a table in front of them. A mechanic was called in to clean and oil the iron heads of the machines, and a carpenter planed the wooden board. Moshe-Avrohom sharpened the knives and scissors and fitted the light hammers with wooden handles. The shop was ready, and whenever Moshe-Avrohom had some free time, he would rush upstairs to sit down and stitch whatever footware he could get. The main thing was not to be idle and to earn a few additional zlotys during the dead winter months.

Chapter 11
GRANDMOTHER HANNAH

When Itte began to feel weak, she decided to inform her brother Mordecai that she would like to have their mother Hannah with her for some time. She will stay at Itte's place, take care of the children, and help out in the household chores as much as she would be able.

Since her husband died and all her children went to live on their own, Hannah had to give up the small store she kept for many years in the village of Sadurki, on the railway line near Lublin. Although two of her children, a son and a daughter, remained in the village, they had to care for their own families and could not help the old mother in her business. Mordecai, Hannah's only son, married a girl from Lublin and settled in a cottage near the railroad station. He was quite successful as a merchant, delivering fresh fruit, living poultry, eggs, or grain to Otwock and other towns on the railway line to Warsaw. Mordecai's sister, Dinah-Leah, who married a cobbler, also remained in Sadurki. However, Hannah's other daughters, Gitel and Itte, settled in faraway cities; Gitel in Warsaw and Itte in Otwock.

As long as Gitel was staying with her, Hannah was able to keep her small cottage with the store where she sold packages of tobacco, writing materials and sometimes, under the counter, a small bottle of vodka. Herself a village woman, she knew well the farmers around and was respected by all, Jews and Poles alike. Still, there were here and there drunks and Jew-baiters who tried to annoy any Jew they could, especially an old widow.

One of these was Hannah's neighbour, Klos. He was a thin, tall Pole with a creased face and red eyes from too much drinking. Klos and his wife were landless peasants and earned their living from working as parobki—hired hands to the better-off farmers. He was often too intoxicated to work and earn his living. When drunk, he firstly took it out on his wife and children. Afterwards, he would come over to Hannah's store, demanding tobacco or merchandise, otherwise he would devastate the place or inform that she sold alcohol without a permit.

Thus, when Gitel left her, Hannah had no choice but to give up the store and go over to live with her children.

At first she moved to Dinah-Leah's place on the other side of the tracks. Here she could sit for hours at the window and observe the outside, or read from her thick prayer-book, with special supplications for women in Yiddish. Outside, beside the cottage, ran the wide unpaved road on which peasants drove their wooden carts, loaded with milk cans and other produce, to the market in the nearby town. Beyond the road, the wheat and barley fields stretched far and wide. To the right, on a hill, stood the wooden windmill whose gray, crossed wings moved slowly in the breeze. To the left, ran the shiny rail-tracks which connected the village with the wide world. On both sides of the tracks were spread in disarray clusters of cottages with plots and barns beside them. Farther on, at the edges of the village, one could distinguish the dark crowns of the apple orchards and nut groves that sprang in abundance on the rich soil of the land.

Nearby, at the other window, sat Berish, Dina-Leah's husband, mending peasants' boots all during the fall and winter. In summer, when the farmers were occupied in the fields and there was little shoe-mending to do, Berish would rent a small orchard and tend it until its fruit were ripe to be picked and sold.

Dinah-Leah was small and feeble, not at all like a country woman. She spoke in a low, hoarse voice, with a sad, complaining intonation. For many years she could not bear any children. Then, in her late thirties, she gave birth to a boy named Chaim, that he may live and grow to adulthood and long life.

And, indeed, Chaim grew up to be a stout and broad-shouldered lad, healthy as a nut, with a red face like the peasant boys around. In summer, he would play and run around with the other Polish children, over the fields and valleys of the village. Together they would swim in the pond behind the windmill or walk, during fall and winter, to the village school. On the way home they loved to skate on the frozen pond or engage in prolonged snowball fights. Although his Polish peers more than once reminded him that he was a Zhidek, a Jewboy, Chaim still remained in good terms with them and did not feel insulted or inferior. He was a strong lad, one of the first in the games and contests and good at school, too. This won him the respect of his peers.

Twice a week, a Hebrew tutor, called Reb Zishe, used to come from the nearby town to teach the children of the few village Jews Hebrew reading and prayers. However, Chaim too often found excuses not to attend or be late at these sessions. He hardly mastered the basics of Hebrew reading, when he refused altogether to meet Reb Zishe. Dinah-Leah's tears and pleadings were to no avail and Berish himself could not dare to lay his hands on his son. The boy was simply too strong-willed and independent to be treated like a child.

It was because of Chaim that Dinah-Leah began to nag her husband to leave the village and settle in Otwock, where her sister Itte dwelled. At first Berish did not give heed to his wife's urgings. He was a village Jew through and through; his father and grandfather were country people—orchard renters, grain merchants, or artisans. He loved the sight of the open fields and the noise and sound of the farm animals. Dressed in a peasant's cotton jacket and high leather boots, he could hardly be distinguished from the Polish farmers from whom he drew his livelihood. Why then should he leave?

However, times were changing, and not for the better. At Hershe's grocery store and inn, where the few village Jews used to meet with merchants from the city, there was a lot of talk about a new enemy of the Jews that had risen in Germany, called Hitler, may his name be obliterated. Inspired by him, local Polish anti-Semites began to incite the unemployed in towns and the landless peasants in the villages to replace the Jewish storekeepers, market vendors, and artisans. In addition to these plagues, it was becoming harder from year to year to earn a living. That summer, there was as usual little shoe work, and the orchard that Berish rented did not turn out well. Meanwhile, Chaim, his only son, continued to run around with his Polish comrades, not giving a thought of settling down or earning a living.

All these troubles and aggravations finally forced Berish to give in to his wife's demand to leave the village. At the end of summer, just before the High Holidays, they packed their belongings on a hired horse-drawn cart and moved to Otwock.

When Dinah-Leah with her husband and son left for Otwock, grandmother Hannah went to live with her son Mordecai and his wife Rachel. Mordecai was engrossed in his business transactions and often had to travel and stay away from home for several days.

Rachel remained at home, taking care of her two children and the house which she furnished with taste and kept sparkling clean. Her free time she spent at the sewing machine, finishing out dresses for the peasant women and the wives of the railway clerks, who appreciated her work greatly and rewarded her with all kinds of produce of the land.

Rachel did not mind having Hannah in her house, if she would only stop reproaching her about the two little daughters, Halina and Marysia. Both girls were fair-haired, with thin braids tied in a coloured band, like the local peasant girls wore. Both of them spoke only Polish, and this irritated Hannah who could hardly communicate with them in her poor and heavily accented Polish. It also pained her that her granddaughters did not receive any Jewish education. Rachel tried to explain to her mother-in-law that nowadays youngsters had to know a perfect Polish, especially when they live in the country, among Poles. But Hannah insisted on hiring the Hebrew tutor so the girls would learn some Hebrew prayers, otherwise they might, God forbid, grow up completely estranged from any Yiddishkeit. Usually, after such an argument, both Rachel and Hannah would go around offended and sulky.

It was at one of those times that Hannah received word from Itte that she is badly needed there to help out in the household. Hannah was glad to see again both Itte and Gitel, her youngest daughter who lived in Warsaw, close to Otwock. Both of them had children, her grandchildren, whom she did not see for a long time. Soon she left by train to Warsaw to stay with Gitel for a short while and move afterwards to her other daughter in Otwock.

Gitel lived in one of the better sections of Warsaw in a spacious three-room apartment whose windows looked out into a paved square enclosed by tall buildings. In the first room was Gitel's husband's furrier shop where he worked frantically, together with his two apprentices, to finish out the fur coats and jackets before the end of the winter season. Afterwards, during the summer, he took it easy, spending the time, together with Gitel and his two children, in a rented cottage somewhere in the country, outside Warsaw.

But here, too, Hannah did not feel quite comfortable. Also Gitel's children, a boy and a girl, were spoken to by their parents and the Polish maid, only in Polish. Hannah felt lonely and forlorn in the big city and was glad to move to her other daughter in Otwock. Here, she finally felt at home. Everyone, grown ups and children, spoke Yiddish and the house was conducted according to Jewish law.

The children in Moshe-Avrohom's household were happy that grandmother Hannah arrived. They surrounded and hugged her and called lovingly, "Bobbe! Dear Bobbe! Good you came to us!" Hannah patted their heads and smiled happily. Small and shrunken, she seemed like another child among her grandchildren. Right away she began to search in her old-fashioned handbag for chocolates and other sweets she brought for the grandchildren.

But even here, in Otwock, Hannah would not remain for long. The workload at her daughter's place was too much for her. She could not stand the noise and shouting of the patrons in the restaurant, and she longed for the serenity of her village. At the end of the summer, when her son Mordecai arrived with merchandise, she packed her bundle and returned with him to Sadurki. Moshe-Avrohom's wife was again left to herself, without a helper.

Chapter 12
IN THE POLISH SCHOOL

When Nohum reached the age of ten, Moshe-Avrohom began to think if he should enroll his son into the Polish public school. Times had changed and nowadays a person had to be able to speak the language of the land and to master other skills, such as reading, writing, and mathematics. None of these were taught in the Heder which Nohum still attended.

Moshe-Avrohom could not make up his mind on this matter for some time. The boy was able and seemed to be studying the Torah eagerly, why then take him away into an entirely different world? On the other hand, Nohum was growing up; pretty soon he will have to learn a trade or help out in the family's business. And whatever he'll become—an artisan or a merchant—the knowledge of Polish and the other subjects that are taught in school will be indispensable. As for his fear that the boy will lose his piety in the new school, there is no guarantee that it will not happen anyways. Nowadays many a youngster comes out a heretic even from a Yeshivah. Thus Moshe-Avrohom and his wife debated with themselves and with each other until they decided to enroll Nohum in public school.

Because he was too old for grade one, Nohum had to be prepared to enter directly into the third grade. He was, therefore, taken out of the old-fashioned Heder of the Baranower and brought into the small, private school of Moshe the Teacher, where both Judaic as well as general subjects were taught.

Moshe the Teacher was a man in his early fifties, tall and slender, with a graying sparse beard. Dressed in a white, clean shirt and a silk vest, with a satin skullcap on his head, he sat at the head of a long wooden table with about a dozen boys of different age seated on both sides. Moshe spoke in a slow, dignified manner that evoked respect towards him. There was no way here to act up or to play dirty tricks against the teacher as at the Baranower's place. The children, too, spoke in hushed voices and walked around on their tiptoes as if not to disturb the serenity of the house. The teacher's wife, a tall woman with a coloured kerchief instead of the traditional wig, moved around quietly, keeping the place clean and watching over her husband. From time to time she placed in front of him a saucer with fruit or a few cookies to refresh himself during his work. At noon, she also served the children cups of sweetened boiled water with milk to drink with the lunches they brought from home.

At Moshe the Teacher's place, no time was spent on talmudic or Hasidic tales and legends, as in the Heder of Yankel of Minsk. After prayers and reviewing the weekly chapter from the Five Books, the serious study of Polish and other secular subjects began. The pupils were divided into twos and threes, one helping the other, while Moshe walked from group to group, correcting and helping out wherever necessary.

Nohum eagerly immersed himself in the new studies, knowing well that on their progress depended his acceptance into the Polish school. By chance this school was across the street, to the rear of the villa where Moshe the Teacher's Heder was. From afar, Nohum could often observe the children running around or playing in the schoolyard during recess. The thought of joining soon this unfamiliar and different place made Nohum somehow uneasy. How will he manage there, still wearing his earlocks and Hasidic attire and knowing so little Polish? Will the other children not mock him and put him to shame? At the same time, Nohum envied the happy and boisterous life of the children out there, and he decided that no matter what, he will succeed and become one of them. When Moshe-Avrohom brought Nohum the day before the beginning of the school year before the Pani Pola, the teacher of grade three, she was not at all pleased with her new pupil.

"To keep a boy till the age of ten in Heder—that's a shame! Not a word of Polish can he pronounce correctly! How do you expect to be treated as equal citizens if you remain Asiaites?" She complained angrily in Moshe-Avrohom's presence.

Moshe-Avrohom controlled himself not to retort to the teacher that it is shameful for a Jewish daughter to utter such words about her own people. He would have added that from the Heder she so berated great men came out—scholars and writers and thinkers. However, he would not be able to say all this in his meager Polish, and, furthermore, he was afraid that he might harm his son's chances of being accepted. Thus he remained silent, waiting what will happen with Nohum who stood beside him scared and shaken from the teacher's sudden outburst. Wholeheartedly he now wanted to pass the examinations and be admitted to the school.

Aware of Nohum's fear, Moshe-Avrohom patted him over the head, whispering in his ears words of encouragement:

"Do not fear, Nohumel, you'll succeed in the studies no worse than others. As for the Heder, there is nothing to be ashamed of it. Great men, writers and scientists, studied in their youth in Heder or Yeshivah. Our Torah is translated and revered all over the world. Be calm, Nohum!"

A warm current of love and pride came over Nohum. With renewed determination he entered the examination room to face Pani Pola. It did not take long and the teacher, with Nohum at her side, came out and announced to Moshe-Avrohom: "Your son, Pan Freidowicz, made it! He passed the exam, in spite of his poor knowledge of Polish. He has the brains."

Moshe-Avrohom thanked her politely and was ready to leave with his son, when Pani Pola added: "He'll be studying in grade three of which I am the home teacher. Tomorrow eight in the morning we'll begin the lessons."

Moshe-Avrohom nodded and Nohum said in Polish:

"Do widzenia, Pani? See you tomorrow!"

"Do widzenia!" Pani Pola replied and turned again to Moshe-Avrohom:

"You may cut off his earlocks. And the black cap of his is also not needed. Here boys wear uniformed caps." Saying this she disappeared among the parents and children that crowded the school corridor.

Next morning, Nohum walked to his new school, carrying on his back a satchel with books and his lunch. The night before, his mother gave him a good hair-washing and shortened his earlocks, so they should not be too much noticed. Along the street, boys and girls carrying briefcases and satchels, streamed towards the Public School Number Four, located right beside the narrow tracks of the small local train from Warsaw to Karczew.

The schoolyard was already full of children of all ages. Many of them walked around in small groups, talking and greeting each other lively. Nohum walked among them, lost and forlorn. He hardly knew anyone and nobody paid attention to him. Soon a man in a navy blue uniform adorned with gilded buttons, appeared and began ringing a large brass bell attached to a wooden handle. Some children ran after him, pulled the tails of his jacket or tried to touch the bell, calling lovingly: "Pan Piotr! Good morning! How are you?"

Pan Piotr put his arm around some of them, patted their heads and urged them to hurry in front of the school entrance where all the grades assembled.

On the steps leading to the school entrance stood several teachers. One of them dressed in a bright sport jacket and trousers, blew a whistle and immediately the children began to line up in pairs according to their grades. The school director, a tall well-groomed man, appeared in the entrance and greeted the teachers. For a while, he stood silently, overlooking the long rows of pupils. Then he nodded to the teacher in the bright jacket who blew the whistle again and commanded: "Attention! The morning prayer!"

The rows straightened.

A powerful song burst from the children's mouths:

> When the morning star appears
> And daytime comes and nears,
> Then sings the earth and the sea;
> Praised, Creator, praised be Thee.

At the back of the line, where Nohum stood among other boys, the singing did not go all well. Some of them did not know the words, others made fun of the ceremony, and whispered jokingly:

"It's prayertime. Let's recite the Eighteen Benedictions!"

The girls in front of the row hushed them softly, "Quiet, boys, quiet!"

Soon the rows of children with their teachers at the head, proceeded into the different classrooms.

All the students of Public School Number Four were exclusively Jewish. Also the staff consisted mainly of Jewish teachers. Only the principal of the school, Pan Szymanski and his wife, were Poles. All of them were united in a common goal—to implant into the children the knowledge and love of the Polish language and its culture. However, this was not an easy task, because nearly all the students came from homes where the traditional Jewish way of life was prevalent. At home, on the streets and courtyards of the Jewish quarter around the bazaar, the children lived and breathed their indigenous Jewish language and culture which became taboo as soon as they entered the school premises. Here, every subject was taught in Polish, the songs, plays, and celebrations—all in Polish. Only one or two hours per week were assigned to the superficial teaching of Jewish history and reli-gion—again in Polish. The Yiddish language was ignored and avoided both in the classroom as in the extra-curricular activities. The children, especially boys, many of whom still attended Heder, found it hard to adjust to the school's regime. They often mingled their Polish with Yiddish words and expressions or sometimes reverted to their native tongue.

Whenever Pani Pola heard a Yiddish word from one of her pupils, she became angry and dismayed.

"What do I hear?" she would exclaim in a pitched voice. "Again the ugly jargon? Here is not a Heder, here is a Polish government school!"

These outbursts did not earn her the children's respect. Behind her back she was mimicked and called mockingly "Pani Perele."

Another type of an assimilated Jew was the drawing and gymnastics teacher, Pan Klar. He grew up in a well-to-do family in Galicia which was part of the Austria-Hungarian Empire before Poland won its independence. There Jews had been emancipated earlier than in tzarist Russia and many of them acquired higher education. Although entirely Polonized, Pan Klar was not ashamed of his Jewish ancestry and even prided himself of his brother, a noted Zionist in Galicia.

Pan Klar was still a bachelor, always well dressed, with a friendly smile on his neatly shaven face. However, from time to time his cheerfulness disappeared and he became angry and irritable. He then walked around silently and morose, and it was dangerous to come close to him. He would slap in the face or beat up with a wooden ruler for the slightest transgression. Luckily, these bouts of anger did not last long; soon he would be back himself, cheerful and approachable, as before. Pan Klar's favourite activities were gymnastics and sports, which he tried to teach zealously to his pupils, especially those of the higher grades. He had served as a corporal in the Polish army and loved military drill. When the weather permitted, he would bring out his class into the schoolyard to exercise under the open sky. Blowing his whistle, he ran after the marching children, commanding:

"Right—left! Down on the ground—rise up! Forward march—with song!"

Arranged in pairs, according to their height, the children marched around the yard singing:

> We are the future of the nation,
> Our chests overflow with strength.

This, as well as other patriotic songs, were taught by the music teacher, Pan Freidman. Although he carried a typically German-Jewish family name, Pan Freidman was thoroughly assimilated and considered himself a Pole in every respect. He grew up and was educated in the Polish culture and it was natural for him to consider that Jews should wholeheartedly integrate into Polish society. As to the mistrust and prejudice of the majority of Poles even towards the fully Polonized Jews, Pan Freidman considered it a temporary phenomenon. An atheist and radical from his youth, he was convinced that sooner or later the Polish working class, in unison with the peasantry and the progressive-minded intelligentsia, will defeat the capitalists and the ruling military clique. Then all social and religious divisions will disappear and the road to full integration will be open, for Jews as for other minorities.

In spite of his leftist convictions, Pan Freidman did not get involved in political activities. He was wholly immersed in the world of music and travelled once a week to Warsaw to further his education at the Conservatory. He also wrote compositions of his own which were left in his desk for the time when the social revolution will open for him new vistas of creative work, according to his ability and potential.

Like Pan Klar, Pan Freidman, too, became sometimes angry and irritated. At such moments he reviled his pupils, slapped their hands and pulled their ears. But as soon as the angry spell left him, he was again composed and friendly, interested in the well-being of every child, especially those from poor families. For their sake, he got involved in a committee of parents and teachers who provided the needy children with a glass of milk and a fresh kaiser roll on the morning recess during the winter months.

The only representative of Judaism in the school was the teacher of Jewish religion, Pan Dutlinger. He was a stout man in his early fifties, learned and steeped in all branches of Judaic lore and wisdom. But all his knowledge was to no avail when he entered the classroom and had to face the children. At that moment, his strength and commanding power left him and he remained at the mercy of his students. He began to walk nervously back and forth in front of the class, reciting in a low voice passages from the great prophets of Israel, the Psalms or the Talmud. From the start nobody listened or paid attention to his words. Some whispered one to another, others were sending written messages to their friends in different corners of the room, or began to do the homework assigned by other teachers.

Pained by the indifference and hostility of the students, Pan Dutlinger began banging his fist on the desk and pointing his forefinger at some of the troublemakers. But to no avail. Some of the boys began to imitate the teacher and thumped on their desk as if they were trying to quieten the others. Some girls joined them calling sanctimoniously, "Quiet! Quiet!" Pan Dutlinger remained silent, waiting patiently until the noise and commotion subsided for a while. He then began anew in his monotonous, sad voice as if pleading for pity and understanding. But the children were engrossed in their misbehaviour and they enjoyed it. Even the usually quiet and shy were emboldened and joined the others in the mischief. Beaten and resigned, Pan Dutlinger stopped trying to control the class; he remained at his desk, waiting for the sound of the school bell to call off his torture.

Suddenly, the door opened and the school director, Pan Szymanski, appeared. He glanced at the pandemonium and began to shout in indignation:

"What's going on here? Are you pupils or a gang of street thugs? It's a shame to treat the teaching of your own religion in such a way!"

Scared and ashamed, the children remained quietly in their seats until the bell rang. Relieved, they hurried out of the classroom and ran down the stairs to the courtyard. Only Pan Dutlinger remained at his desk to rest for a while before he headed to his next teaching assignment.

Chapter 13
IN TRANSITION

During the first months, Nohum felt quite uncomfortable in the new school. Whenever he forgot himself and uttered a word in Yiddish, Pani Pola rebuked him again and again. From Pan Klar he, more than once, was slapped and even once badly beaten. It happened during one of the art lessons when pupils were allowed to share their colour pencils and drawing material. For the slothful, this was an ideal occasion to indulge in all kind of time-wasting, as sending notes or drawing frivolous pictures. It happened when the commotion was too much for him, Pan Klar lost his temper and began pacing nervously between the rows, looking for someone to take out his ire, and, thus, set an example for others. Once, in such an agitated state, he noticed that Nohum was scribbling with his pencil on the shiny surface of the desk instead of a sheet of paper. He ran over to Nohum and began striking him with the wooden ruler wherever he could. The beating was so severe that Nohum had to remain home several days until he got over it.

The uncrowned king in class, beside the teacher, was a ruffian named Velvel Davidowicz. He was a heavy-set, tough boy, with protruding teeth in a cynical, nasty smile. He was the son of a market vendor and from his childhood he had learned the slang and foul language of the street people. The girls feared and avoided him because he used to pinch them, pull their braids, and utter words which made their faces red with shame. Also the boys were afraid of him and of his two or three comrades who surrounded him and fulfilled all his whims.

On winter days, when the children were allowed to stay inside during recess, Velvel would sit on top of a desk and command:

"You, Komar, run and bring me a bagel from the woman vendor at the school gate. And you, Marek, place the broom behind the door, so it will hit the religious teacher when he enters the class. And you, little Nohum, must help me write the assignment on King Casimir the Yagellon, damned be his father and father's father!"

Although Nohum was not one of the strong boys in class, he was somehow favoured by Velvel who took him under his protection and did not allow anybody to harm him.

A year had passed and Nohum advanced into grade four. He made great progress in mastering the Polish language and was beginning to read and appreciate some of the writings of the Polish poets and prose masters. His written assignments earned high marks from Pani Szymanska, the teacher of Polish, and the school director's wife. More than once she read some of his essays to the class and afterwards displayed them on the classroom board. For some time Nohum continued to attend in the afternoon Moshe the Teacher's Heder. But soon his parents realized that it is too hard for the boy to study from morning till afternoon in Public School, and afterwards, till evening, in Heder. In addition, Nohum had to do, after supper, his readings and written assignments for the Polish school. "We cannot exhaust the child," Itte argued. "He is so frail and has to study so much in school and at home."

Moshe-Avrohom was silent, but his wife persisted:

"What do you want? Nohumel knows well all the prayers and is fluent in the Five Books. If other children would know as much as him, their parents would be happy. Furthermore, we cannot afford to pay so high a tuition to Moshe the Teacher! He's expensive like a druggist." Moshe-Avrohom realized that his wife was right. As the sages say, one sin causes another one. Since he enrolled his son in the Polish school, he will have to forgo Heder. You cannot dance at two weddings at the same time. Still, he could not let his son interrupt completely his Judaic studies. So he arranged with Reb Shmuel, a sage who spent his days in the House of Study, to tutor Nohum in the Talmud just on Monday and Thursday afternoons for a small fee.

Free from the yoke of Heder, Nohum became a full-fledged schoolboy, like everyone else. His earlocks disappeared and he persuaded his father to buy him a school cap with a shiny black visor and a small Polish eagle on top. Now Nohum wore his dark Jewish cap and gaberdine only when he attended his Talmud lessons in the House of Study, or Saturday morning, when he walked with his father to the morning service at the Bikkur Holim Society.

Nohum could now remain after classes in the schoolyard and participate in games and other extra-curricular activities. The most popular game was 'Between Two Fires'. The players were divided into two teams, each with its captain and its assigned portion of the field. The ball was then thrown from the captain to his team members over the heads of the competing children. When the captain or one of his boys succeeded in hitting anyone from the opposite team, the player was disqualified and had to leave the field. The players ran wildly in the marked areas, trying to avoid being hit by the ball. The game ended when all the participants of one group were smitten and removed from their territory. During the match, the clamor and excitement of the participants and the onlookers was great. Often noisy quarrels broke out between the competing groups, until one of the teachers, or Piotr, the janitor, came out to remind them that it's time to leave for home.

It also happened that the boys went right from school to a nearby field to train for a forthcoming competition with one of the other public schools in town. Exhausted from running around and yelling, the boys lay down on the grass and rested. When hungry, they collected the remnants from their lunches and snacks and divided them equally among all. Often they pitched in their pocket money and sent out someone to buy a snack for the bunch. Once such a messenger returned with a bag of fresh rolls and a large pork sausage. "It's kosher like a pig's tail," he said with a chuckle. He then handed out the rolls and the cut up chunks of Kielbasa. Nohum picked his portion and began to bite the roll, but could not put the slice of sausage into his mouth. The detested smell of pork which hit him whenever he passed Gaiger's meat shop on Bazaar Street made him nauseated and close to vomiting. Velvel, the gang-leader, got up and faced Nohum, commanding:

"Swallow it right now, or you get it straight in the kisser!"

The boys got up and circled Nohum, watching how he chewed unwillingly the roll with the goyish meat.

Next day, in the afternoon, sitting in the House of Study with Reb Shmuel, Nohum was upset and disconcerted. He could not forget what had happened in the field the day before. He tasted 'trefes', pork meat, how can he now sit in the House of Study at the open volume of the Gemara? He will repent, Nohum heartened himself, he is not yet thirteen years old, when one is punished for his transgressions. At the same time, he doubted if his sin was really noticed above, in heaven. How could it be that every minute action here on earth is accounted there? Maybe all the tales of Paradise and Gehenna were made up by the Rabbis to scare the people into submission? Nohum did not believe anymore in ghosts and demons, only in the One Above. However, some of his school friends argued that there is no God; everything proceeds by the laws of nature. How could it be—such a tremendous universe without a Master?

Reb Shmuel, Nohum's tutor, inhaled another pinch of snuff from his silver snuffbox and began to recite aloud a legal dispute about the responsibilities of an unpaid keeper in case the things that were left with him were stolen or damaged. Nohum joined Reb Shmuel in the reciting of the text, and moved with him back and forth, but the deliberations of the Rabbi's were far from his mind. He found it hard to follow the hair-splitting argumentations of the ancient scholars and hoped that they will hit on a more interesting passage—a legend or anecdotal story about one of the sages.

At home, Nohum still conducted himself properly; he recited his prayers every morning and evening, and attended with his father the Saturday morning service. Friday night, after the Sabbath meal, often Nohum accompanied his father to the large modern synagogue on Warsaw Street, in the upper part of the city. Its main sanctuary was adorned with brightly lit chandeliers and an elaborately decorated Holy Ark. The benches there were of dark varnished wood and the floor smooth and clean. Two rows of columns on both sides of the hall supported parallel balconies for the women. The synagogue was built and supported by a wealthy benefactor, a merchant from Petersburg, who settled in Otwock after the Bolshevik revolution. He furthermore engaged a half a dozen young scholars from Lithuanian Talmudic academies, some of them married and with children, to keep the flame of Torah alive all year round. In the smaller chapel of the synagogue, some of these erudites gave, on Friday night, discourses for laymen on the weekly portion of the Torah. In their Lithuanian Yiddish, they reviewed the weekly portion from the Five Books, often actualizing it in the light of political and social issues of the day.

On the way home, Moshe-Avrohom walked leisurely, still inspired by the words of the young scholar. Nohum walked beside him, silent and morose. He recalled the moralizing words of the preacher and felt guilty and sinful. In the school, among his classmates, life was free, with no prohibitions and minute obligations to fulfill. But there, in the synagogue, he felt a mysterious beauty, a holiness that made life somehow more meaningful.

With the coming of spring, Nohum was carried away even more with the life of the school. During the month of May, Nohum's school friends used to arrange Saturday outings way beyond the city, to the site where the Swider River entered the Vistula, or to the abandoned castle in Old Otwock. There the boys sang and pranced, played games, and shared picnic meals. Sometimes they were attacked by Polish youngsters and had to flee, but this didn't keep them back from new outings.

Nohum heard so much about these adventurous excursions that he desired, at least once, to experience one of them. But how could he when he had to be every Saturday, from morning till noontime, with his father at the prayer service? Afterwards, there was usual-ly a Kiddush—a wine and cake reception—on the spot or in one of the member's houses, at which the congregants socialized and lingered for some time. Then, when they returned home, the Sabbath meal began, with singing and reciting the Grace after Meals. By the time it was all over, the best part of the day was gone.

Once the boys decided to view a soccer match on a Saturday afternoon. It was supposed to be a contest between a representation of the two Jewish sport clubs—the Zionist "Hapoel" joined with the leftist "Vulcan"—on one hand, and the Polish O.K.S.—the "Otwock Sport Club"—on the other.

On that afternoon, right after the meal, Nohum, still in his Sabbath gaberdine and cap, sneaked out of the house to meet his comrades in front of the school. From there they proceeded along Karczew Street to the Warsaw highway. There, beyond the highway, was the soccer field with gates of twisted wire on both sides.

As the boys approached the field, they got excited and began to race towards it. When Nohum reached the field, he began to walk along its marked borderline where many onlookers had congre-gated. On the large rectangular playfield, junior soccer players from the three clubs were filling out the time before the real match. The people around did not pay too much attention to the ongoing game. They walked leisurely or assembled in small groups, discussing the forthcoming match. More people were con-stantly arriving, swelling the ranks of the spectators. It seemed that all the youth of Otwock—Jews and Poles --were gathering to witness the contest of the two teams. Here were youngsters from the different Zionist youth organizations—the 'Hechalutz', 'Hash-omer Hatzair' and 'Betar'—all in their unique blouses and ties. In other spots, members and sympathizers of the left-wing Workers' Union or separate groups of porters, butcher-boys, and other "tough guys" gathered.

Soon Nohum lost his schoolmates and continued to stroll by himself around the field, eagerly observing all and everything. For the first time in his life he saw so many young people, boys and girls, enjoying themselves so freely and unrestrainedly on a Saturday—the day of holiness and rest.

The Junior's match ended and the crowd stretched itself along both sides of the field to greet the arriving teams. They came from opposite sides and met each other in the middle of the field. The O.K.S. players were dressed in white short-sleeved shirts, with black emblems of their club, and in red shorts with green bands on both sides. The Jewish footballists wore all the 'Hechalutz' outfit—blue blouses and white shorts. The players of both teams were all young and sturdy fellows, some broad-shouldered and stout, others tall and lean, all with muscular bodies and sunburnt faces.

For a while both teams stood silently, facing one another; then the captains came forward and greeted each other with hand-shakes. From somewhere appeared the referee, dressed in a white shirt, with a black necktie, and light trousers. He blew the whistle and the game began. The players positioned themselves in their places and the two goalkeepers stood attentively at the goal mouths. In front of them, to the right and left, were the defenders, and in center—the attackers of both teams. Swiftly they rushed over the field, kicking the ball with their heavy boots, skillfully avoiding their opponents. They carried the ball some distance, transferring it to one of their own, closer to the rival's goal. The O.K.S. players were attacking, carrying the ball towards the Jewish goalkeeper. The Jewish onlookers became excited and began to encourage aloud their footballists: "Goalkeeper, be ready! Boys, start working! Left defender, take over the ball!"

A tall guy from the Polish team was in front of the gate, ready to shoot the ball inside, when Yankele Shtern, one of the best Jewish players, appeared from behind and stole the ball. All around shouted with delight: "Bravo, Yankele, bravo! Shake him, turn him around!"

Encouraged by the ovation, Yankele turned nimbly around the O.K.S. player, not losing the ball.

"Don't play too much, Yankele!" the callers instructed him from afar. "Pass it forward!"

Yankele sprang forward, the ball rolling ahead of him. A few of his comrades rushed along, flanking him from both sides. In seconds they were at the goal of the Poles. The goalkeeper ran forward to snatch the ball from under Yankele's feet. But it was too late. In an instant Yankele managed to send over the ball to a teammate on the left who shot it right into the wire net.

The Jews rejoiced wildly, yelling "Hurrah! A goal!" Some jumped for joy, others embraced one another or shook hands.

The referee threw the ball and the match began anew. The O.K.S. players were now determined not to allow the Jews to win. Now they carried the ball steadily forward, showing off and hitting it with their heads, until they, too, managed to score a goal. The match began anew. Both teams tried to attack and to show off their mastery and proficiency. At the end, the Poles won, two against one.

On the way home, all excitedly discussed the highlights of the match. Although the Poles won, there was nothing to be ashamed of—the Jewish team played well and showed themselves as worthy opponents of the first class Polish club.

Soon the crowd of players and their fans were on Karczew Street, where they had to pass by the Parisover Rabbi's courtyard. The old Rabbi had passed away not long ago and his son, barely seventeen years old, had been married off and crowned as the new head of the dynasty. Followers from all over Poland had come to witness the event and some lingered on around the Rabbi's courtyard. It was the hour between the afternoon and the evening prayers and many Hasidim congregated in front of the gate. With sad eyes they followed the passing crowd of Jewish youth who so openly desecrated the holy Sabbath.

Nohum walked in the throng with his gaberdine folded in his hands and without his cap. In the commotion, when the match was over, a Polish lad grabbed it and threw it on top of the wired football goal. Nohum did not try to retrieve it; somehow he was glad to get rid of it and not to wear it anymore.

Slowly and carefully he sneaked into his courtyard, hoping that nobody would notice him. But, as soon as he entered the yard,

Leibel, the landlord's adopted son, appeared before him, dressed in full Sabbath attire—a belted silk gaberdine and brown fur hat with points around the rim. Leibel stared in disbelief at Nohum and called: "Oy gevald! Is this Nohum? Without a headcover, all sweating? So soon spoiled!"

Nohum tore himself away as if singed and ran as quickly as he could up the hall staircase to his apartment.

Chapter 14
THE WRITTEN ASSIGNMENT

Nohum had studied in the Polish school for four years until he had reached grade seven—the last year in the public school. By then he was one of the top students in class, especially in the humanities—Polish Language, Literature, and History. Pani Szymanska, the school director's wife, who taught Polish language and literature in the higher grades, appreciated Nohum's well-written compositions and his genuine interest in the subject.

The latest composition Pani Szymanska had assigned was entitled "What will I do after graduating from public school?" In her usual, quiet manner, she elaborated that only six months remained till the end of this final school year, and it's time to think seriously what each of you will do afterwards. A few may go on studying in high school; others will probably go into apprenticeships and learn a trade or help out in their family businesses. Thus, each one will have to find his own niche in life and become independent and useful to himself and to society. The home assignment will undoubtedly force everyone to ponder and clarify his thoughts on such an important and vital issue.

Nohum delayed the writing of the composition until the day before it was due to be handed in. Although he knew well that Pani Szymanska was strict in such matters, he could not help himself and kept on postponing the writing from day to day. But now it had to be done, no matter what.

After school, Nohum hurried into the family's restaurant for his meal and then to the apartment on the second floor, where he would be able to work in peace. The two room flat upstairs looked abandoned and neglected. Gray cobwebs hung in the corners under the ceiling; the tiled stove stood unused and covered with old newspapers; and Father's stitching machines were cluttered with old leather cuts and tools. Nohum sat down beside the wide window sill and placed his writing book and ink pen before him. Outside, the sky was overcast and a thin, nasty rain began rapping on the window-panes of the hunched houses on the street. Through the uncurtained windows, Nohum could distinguish the silhouettes of the neighbours from across the street: the Deaf Shoemaker, the Little Tailor, Godel the Tinsmith, and Zanvele the Cobbler—all engaged in their daily work.

"What will happen with my assignment?" Nohum asked himself. It has to be delivered tomorrow during the first hour in class, and he had not yet written even one line!

Nohum glanced at the empty page of his composition book, with only the title of the assignment on its top. Indeed, what is he going to do with himself after school is over? He is no longer a child; in three months from now he will turn fourteen and soon afterwards he will graduate from school.

Deep inside, Nohum believed that he is able and should continue his studies in high school and later on—at university. He loved to read and was eager to devote himself to the study of history, literature, and art. However, he knew well that all his aspirations were unachievable dreams. His father and mother laboured all year round, from early morning till late at night—and they could hardly feed the family and pay the rent for the restaurant and the rooms upstairs. How can he even think of enrolling in high school, when the fee alone amounts to twenty or more zlotys per month, not including textbooks, the uniform, and other expenses? Who will support him another four years until he'll complete the course of studies? And how will he proceed afterwards at university? Already last year, Father suggested that Nohum should quit school and begin an apprenticeship with one of the artisans in the neighbourhood.

The thought that he'll soon have to spend his days bent over a sewing machine or a shoemaker's table filled Nohum with dread. He had read many books by Jules Verne, Karl May, and Ossendowski which told about faraway, exotic places, daring expeditions and adventures. More than once he had daydreamed about leaving home and setting out on his own into the wide world. Once he even tried, together with a school friend, to realize such an adventurous dream.

It happened last year, during the long summer vacation, when children were allowed to travel by train all over Poland, provided they were accompanied by an adult passenger. Without notifying their parents, Nohum and his friend packed their knapsacks and left for the railway station. After soliciting several passengers at the ticket window, they found a traveller who got them free tickets to Lublin.

For several days the two youngsters trudged the streets of Lublin, visiting old synagogues and the famous Yeshiva of the Sages of Lublin. Afterwards, Nohum suggested they go to the village of Sadurki, only a few train stops from Lublin, where Grandma Hannah and the other relatives lived. Here they stayed a few days at Uncle Mordecai's place, and visited Uncle Berish and Cousin Chaim in their summer orchard not far from the village. Meanwhile, Uncle Mordecai notified Nohum's parents on the whereabouts of the boys and he was urged to send them back home. Tired and worn out, Nohum and his companion returned to Otwock, now realizing that it is not so easy and simple to set out on their own into the wide world.

Nohum left his place at the window and began to pace back and forth, telling himself that he must not give up or lose his courage. He then returned to his place and began to write.

"It's nearly five years since I began to study in our school. When I entered grade three, I was barely ten years old, and now I am a young man on the threshold of a new life, outside the protective walls of the school.

"All these years I was a diligent student, and I passed from grade to grade with high marks. I am grateful to my teachers for the knowledge and values they instilled and for the genuine curiosity they awoke in me. I am keenly interested in all subjects that deal with man's spiritual life and his literary and artistic achievements. I am eager to continue to study in high school and, later on, at university. I dream of becoming a scholar, a writer, who would use his talent and knowledge for the benefit of the poor and downtrodden in our midst.

"However, all these ambitions of mine are hollow dreams, because to continue studying, one needs well-to-do parents or patrons who will support you. Unfortunately, I am a child of poor, hard-working people who have to feed and clothe four more children, beside me, and I, the oldest, am obliged to do my share and help them.

"But where should I proceed and what should I do? For me all venues of proper employment are barred. I am a second class citizen in my homeland which I love and whose culture I admire. Yet I am not considered a legitimate son of Poland, but a stepchild on the Vistula. I am discriminated against when seeking employment at any government office or enterprise; I am insulted and reviled on the streets by Polish hooligans; I'm treated unjustly both as a Jew and as a child of poor parents."

Nohum stopped for a while to re-read what he had written. "What am I writing?" he asked himself. "They might even expel me for that..." But no! He cannot be silenced, he must express what grieves him so deeply. Nohum took again the pen in his ink-stained fingers and continued to write.

"I am now at the crossroads of my young life. The carefree school years are soon over, and I have no prospects for a decent future. I see so many young, unemployed men and women around, all of them denied a proper place in life. It seems to me the world is a jungle where one has to fight desperately for existence, with no regard for the well-being of others. It seems to me also that everything we were taught in school, all that we read in books, is of a fairy-tale reality. In the real world naked force prevails, the strong devour the weak, as in the animal kingdom.

"So where will I go and what will I do after graduation? I really do not know! But one thing I do know: wherever I'll be and whatever I'll do, I will always be with the poor, oppressed and exploited! With them I'll struggle for a better tomorrow for all working people, for a life worth living."

Late at night Nohum lay on his cot and could not fall asleep. It was dark and humid in the room where the whole family slept. Father and mother lay in the joined beds with the two younger children, and the two sisters were together on a folding mattress on the floor. Nohum thought about his written assignment which would have to be handed in in the morning. He pondered about his life and future and accused himself of being weak, of giving up too easily. He should not agree to become a shoemaker or a tailor, as most of the youngsters around have done. He is young and able, and should strive and suffer to achieve his goals. This is the road others took and, sooner or later, succeeded.

Exhausted, Nohum finally fell asleep.

He was awakened by his mother who stood over him and spoke lovingly: "Nohumel, it's late! You'll be late to school!"

Nohum opened his eyes, smiled to his mother and called out: "Right away, Mame! I'll be ready in a few minutes!"

He jumped down, washed and dressed speedily, grabbed his lunch, and was soon on the way to school.

On Bazaar Street, along which Nohum walked hurriedly, stores were being opened. Elderly Jews, with prayer-shawl bags under arms, hurried to the nearby synagogue; farmers were arriving with their produce on horse-driven carts. Beside the opened bazaar-stands stood the merchant women, wrapped in dark shawls, ready to begin the daily struggle for existence. After a short while, the bazaar and market area were behind him; he passed the firemen's hall with its fenced yard through which he could already see the school. The bell was ringing when he ran into the school-yard and the class rows in front of the entrance were already formed. Nohum managed to reach his group and attach himself to its end.

In class, the children rose from their seats as Pani Szymanska entered. She was a tall, blonde woman, with red make-up on her cheeks, and light-blue, lively eyes. Behind her walked the school director, Pani Szymanska's husband, carrying her leather briefcase, which he left on the floor, beside her desk. The children pulled out their writing books and began to whisper one to another about their assignments. Pani Szymanska lifted her head from over the class-register and her sharp, strict glance hushed the class immediately. The teacher began to call out the names of the children in alphabetical order, and each pupil came over and left his writing book on her desk. Nohum's heart began to beat faster when he heard his name. As he put down his writing book, Pani Szymanska greeted him with a smile. Nohum returned to his seat relieved. "Let it be what might be", he said to himself.

The same afternoon, Pani Szymanska sat at the desk in her living room and read the assignments of her grade seven pupils. With a sharpened red pencil she corrected the spelling mistakes and rearranged the faulty sentence structures of the compositions. When Pani Szymanska began to read Nohum's composition, she slowed down to read and re-read its content. A light, sarcastic smile appeared on her lips when she laid the writing book aside to show it to her husband. Soon Pan Szymanski came in from his office which was next door to their apartment, and his wife handed him Nohum's composition book, saying: "Please, Wladziu, read this..."

The school director sat down on the nearby sofa with Nohum's writing book in hand. After glancing over the few pages, he exclaimed:

"As I love God! This one writes like a Communist! A real Communist!"

Pan Szymanski was both disturbed and saddened by the boy's writing. It caused him once more to reflect on the Jewish Question in Poland. He did not consider himself at all an anti-Semite. He was appalled by the brutal excesses against Jews which had occurred lately here and there. In his dealings with the children's parents who came for all kinds of reasons to his office, he was always correct and friendly. Most of them spoke in a mutilated, heavily accented Polish, but Pan Szymanski answered their inquiries with patience and without condescension. He was, therefore, considered by the parents to be friendly, inclined to Jews, not an Enemy of Israel, in any event.

Over the years, Pan Szymanski had become intrigued by his work among Jews. He saw them as they were—poor and hard-working people, struggling to eke out a livelihood from their small stores and shops. He also admired their striving to educate, and thus improve the lot of their children. However, he soon learned that the Jews are a close-knit ethnic people with its own religion, language, and way of life to which they were strongly attached.

As a Polish patriot, Pan Szymanski believed that Poland needs unity and inner strength to withstand the pressures of her mighty neighbours—the Russians to the east, and the Germans to the west. The Jews did not fit well into this scheme. He would rather have them emigrate to Palestine or overseas, to the Americas, where their brethren live and prosper. Perhaps by the time Poland had only a few hundred thousand Jews, instead of over three million, the problem would become manageable. As in Western Europe, they would become enlightened and productive citizens, Poles of Mosaic faith. Still, as an educator, entrusted by the Ministry with a school of several hundred children, all of them Jewish, he saw it as his duty to educate them in the spirit of Polish patriotism and culture and to uproot their backward superstitions and habits. He began his efforts by teaching cleanliness and good manners. Thus the children were instructed to appear in school with washed and combed heads, wearing clean shirts and blouses, and in shined up footware. His next task was to bar the Yiddish tongue, so it should not be heard neither in the classrooms nor in the schoolyard. Afterwards, Pan Szymanski introduced the morning prayer at the beginning of the day—a general prayer which was neither Jewish nor Catholic.

Beside these innovations, Pan Szymanski strove to raise the patriotic spirit in the school. The walls of the classrooms were adorned with the portraits of the national leaders, the Marshal Pilsudski and President Moscicki. All national holidays, such as Independence Day or the anniversary of the May Constitution, were celebrated with school assemblies. In addition, there were occasional visits to the synagogue on Warsaw Street, to hear patriotic sermons and prayers for the well-being of the Republic by the officiating city Rabbi. Pan Freidman, the music teacher, was instructed to teach more songs in praise of Poland's earth, sea and mountains. From his office window, Pan Szymanski often looked down upon the children marching under Pan Klar's command, singing aloud in Polish. This gave him a feeling of pride and achievement.

However, on occasions like these, after reading Nohum's essay, Pan Szymanski had serious doubts as to the effectiveness of his life's work. True, inside the school, he managed to create a genuine Polish atmosphere, he succeeded in nurturing the children's respect and love for the Fatherland. But as soon as they left school, they retreated into the self-imposed Jewish ghetto. There, they filled the ranks of the Jewish nationalist youth organization, the Zionists, the Socialists, and, worst of all—the Communists, the sworn enemies of Poland.

Lately, after the death of Marshal Jozef Pilsudski, the country was deeply troubled by disorder and violence. Strikes and anti-government demonstrations multiplied in the cities, peasant rebellions erupted in the eastern regions of the country, often followed by bloody pacifications. All of these were both exploited and directed by the well-organized underground Communist Party, and supported by Moscow. True, the Polish Secret Police was quite effective, making arrests and arranging political trials which ended with heavy prison terms for the perpetrators. But all these measures did not bring an end to the political turmoil in the country. Pan Szymanski, like any other patriotic-minded Polish intellectual, lived with these events and looked for a way to solve the difficult problems of his homeland. Now, after reading Nohum's assignment, he felt deeply disturbed. It was a sure indication that here, too, in his domain, something was rotten.

And whom could he blame if not Pan Perelmuter, the new religion teacher who replaced a year ago the ailing Pan Dutlinger? He, this insolent young man, must be one of those Communist agitators that was inserted into his school to corrupt the minds of the children of the higher grades. He, Pan Szymanski, suspected this for some time, while observing the new teacher's demeanor, his intimate talks and discussions he often conducted in the classroom, or during recess, in the courtyard. Moreover, he is disregarding quite openly the accepted practice not to use the Yiddish language on the school premises. Already several times he has overheard him reading from Yiddish books during class sessions. Something has to be done against this effrontery. And the sooner—the better...

Chapter 15
THE NEW TEACHER

Next morning, at the first recess, Nohum was called into the director's office. Scared and nervous, he knocked at the door and entered. There, behind a large oak desk adorned with a marble ink-set, sat Pan Szymanski, silent and stern-looking. "Where did you get the ideas you expressed in your home assignment?" demanded Pan Szymanski, looking straight at Nohum. With his head down, Nohum stood still, at a loss to find an answer. Raising his voice, Pan Szymanski continued:

"Who put these ideas in your head? Didn't you discuss these matters during the religion sessions with Pan Perlmuter? Tell the truth, and nothing will happen to you!"

Nohum could not withstand the pressure anymore and he began to cry and stammer:

"I wrote the assignment myself...nobody told me anything...With Pan Perlmuter we study only religion..."

Saying this, Nohum felt relieved—he had not betrayed his beloved teacher. Pan Szymanski continued for a while his investigation, alternating polite questions with threats of expulsion from school. Finally, the director lost his patience and ordered abruptly: "March home! Come back with your father!"

An hour later, Nohum returned into Pan Szymanski's office with his father beside him. The director ordered Nohum to wait in the corridor, and then invited Moshe-Avrohom to sit down.

"Your son, Pan Freidowicz," Pan Szymanski began, "is an able boy, one of the best students in class. But I suspect that he has fallen under an undesirable influence. You are probably aware of the times in which we live. The external and internal enemies of our land are raising their heads. Our young people are especially vulnerable, because their idealism could be easily exploited by all kinds of radical demagogues. You have to watch the boy that he not become involved with them, otherwise he'll cause you a lot of grief and trouble..." Moshe-Avrohom nodded, showing that he understood the seriousness of the matter.

"I'll forgive him this time," said Pan Szymanski, "because of you. I know you are an honest, hard-working man. But remember—watch your son. The less he will have to do with politics, the better for him."

Out in the schoolyard, Moshe-Avrohom reproached Nohum:

"Was it worthwhile, with your writing, to get into so much trouble?"

"But I wrote only the truth, Father!" Nohum tried to justify himself. Moshe-Avrohom answered sadly: "For the truth, you get a beating."

Since Pan Perlmuter, the new religion teacher, replaced Pan Dutlinger, an amazing change occurred in the higher grades of the school. For years, Pan Dutlinger had struggled in vain to win the children's goodwill and cooperation. Each year classes changed, but the unhappy state of affairs remained. Pan Dutlinger kept on reciting the lofty words of Israel's ancient prophets, or retelling the lives and deeds of the talmudic sages—always in front of an indifferent, hostile class.

In the end, Pan Dutlinger fell sick and had to give up teaching. At the beginning of the school year, in grade six, a new religion teacher appeared in Nohum's class. He was a young man, in his higher twenties, tall and muscular, dressed in a zippered khaki blouse and in bright sport trousers. Amazed to see this kind of religion teacher, the children fell silent and waited. Introducing himself, Pan Perlmuter took out a book from his briefcase, and began to read a story by I.L. Peretz, in Yiddish.

It was the first time that the children had heard a teacher in this school reading or speaking in their familiar language. It intrigued them and they listened attentively to the story of an old messenger lost on a stormy winter night. After the reading, a discussion on the content and meaning of the story ensued. From the start, the children were charmed by the carefree manner of the new teacher and by the novel material he introduced. The reading of Yiddish short stories and poems continued on the following lessons and the children learned the names and biographies of many writers and poets they had never heard of before.

The scope of the lively discussions, in Polish and in Yiddish, following the readings, slowly broadened to include current political issues and events: the rise of anti-Semitism in Poland, events in Palestine, the Soviet Union, and elsewhere. A core of interested boys and girls gathered around the new teacher and followed him even during recess in the schoolyard or in the classroom. Pan Perlmuter listened attentively to everyone's questions and probings, guiding and helping them to find by themselves the right answers and conclusions. Some boys wondered as to what ideology or political movement the new teacher was attached. Moshe Gelman, one of the older ones in the group and an ardent "leftist", told them confidentially, "He must be one of our own—a left-winger..."

It did not take long before the conduct of the new religion teacher drew the attention of the school director. Entering by chance one of Pan Perlmuter's sessions, he could notice the sudden interruption of the reading or discussion. He noticed as well, Pan Perlmuter's prolonged conversations with some of the pupils during recess or when classes were dismissed.

Now, after reading Nohum's assignment and questioning him in the office, it became clear to Pan Szymanski that no other than the new religion teacher was responsible for the radical ideas of some of the students of grade seven. That young man must be either a convinced Communist, or even a party member, sent into the school to indoctrinate the youngsters and recruit some of them into the Communist Youth League. Pan Szymanski made up his mind to fire the teacher as soon as the school year was over, or before that, if possible. Meanwhile, he will keep his eyes open and quietly gather the evidence against him.

These were hard and trying times for the over three million Jews of Poland. Faced with an aggravating political and economic crisis, the rulers of the land decided upon a policy of political and economic discrimination against the Jews. Jewish ritual slaughter, which provided a livelihood for thousands—slaughterers, supervisors, and butchers -- was under constant attack and in danger of being outlawed by the Polish parliament. Landless peasants were urged to take over the stores and market stands from the Jews. Agitators appeared in the bazaars and markets with the slogan of 'each one to his own', which meant that Poles should buy only from Polish merchants. In the universities and other higher learning institutions, Jewish students were forced to occupy special left-side benches. The students protested by attending the lessons standing. Three years after Hitler became the ruler of Germany, the venomous racial theories and the obnoxious deeds of the Nazis found a following in neighbouring Poland. Physical attacks on Jews multiplied on the campuses and on the streets of many cities.

And then, in 1936, a pogrom occurred in the town of Przytyk. Crowds, incited by agitators, attacked the Jewish quarter, and plundered their property. Many Jews were wounded and a few murdered. The police arrived too late and arrested some of the attackers as well as those Jews who tried to defend themselves. The reports of these events filled the pages of the Yiddish dailies and they were discussed everywhere—at home, on the streets, and in school.

A few blocks from Nohum's school was the Wladislaw Reymont Public School, for Polish children exclusively. In general, there was little cooperation between the two schools, except for sport events that were arranged from time to time by the gymnastics teachers of both institutions. Lately however, all friendly contact stopped and open hostility became the rule.

One afternoon, when the classes in Nohum's school were dismissed and groups of pupils began to leave the building, they were greeted by a hail of stones. A gang of Polish youngsters blocked the school gate; others were positioned in corners behind the wooden fence—all armed with stones and sticks, ready to attack the Jewish children.

"Come out Jewboys! Come out Beilises! Let's have a fight!" they challenged from afar.

The Jewish children retreated in panic behind the school building. Those who were hit by stones, or were simply scared, broke into loud crying. Suddenly, Moshe Gelman rushed forward, shouting:

"Cowards! Milksops! Fainthearted Jews! Don't run away! Let's pay them back!" With a few stones in hand, he ran towards the gate, and after him followed a few of the more daring boys. Stones began to fly back and forth, along with war cries and insults.

Soon the school director and some of the teachers came down to find out what was going on. The children surrounded them, telling excitedly of the unprovoked assault. The attackers showed little respect or fear for the teachers, reviling and swearing at them:

"Away with you, Jewish hirelings! Away, Judases!"

Pan Szymanski stood silent for a while, deeply shaken from what he saw and heard. He recovered shortly, ordered the children to retreat deeper into the schoolyard and went to his office to inform the police. Somehow the Polish youngsters got wind of it and dispersed before the arrival of the two policemen.

For days after this event the pupils in Nohum's school talked and commented on what had happened. In grade seven, during the religion sessions with Pan Perlmuter, they discussed heatedly the proper solution to the Jewish Question—Zionism or Socialism. Pan Perlmuter sat on the edge of his desk, looking at the faces of the more than thirty boys and girls whose lively, curious eyes were all directed at him. In his neat sport blazer, he looked like one of them, an older comrade engaged in a friendly get-together.

The class was considering a much publicized story of a Warsaw lawyer, Ripel by name, who called for a mass exodus of Jews from Poland. In his announcements in the press, Ripel suggested that Jews, with their families and all the belongings they can carry with them, should march to the Land of Israel, as they did in the Exodus from Egypt. Some of the students were amused; others were intrigued by this unusual and desperate plan. But Moshe Gelman, the leftist, stood up and exclaimed:

"It's a scandal! The man must be out of his wits! We must stay put here and fight for a better life, and not wander all over the world!"

Nohum disagreed, pointing out that such a dramatic mass exodus might arouse the world to the plight of the Jews in Poland. And maybe the people would indeed reach, after much suffering and travail, the shores of Palestine.

Since Shaindel, his sister, had left for Hachsharah, Nohum had remained under the spell of the Zionist ideal she had kindled in him. Shaindel's unflinching belief in a new beginning, that she and her like would make in the ancient Jewish land, inspired him. He read eagerly her letters and the Zionist pamphlets she left at home. Thus Nohum became the spokesman for the Zionist cause during the class discussions.

Pan Perlmuter would listen attentively to Nohum's reasoning and then refute one by one all his assumptions. Palestine, he argued, is a small stretch of land settled with an indigenous Arab population that resided there for generations. In order to become a majority, the Jews would have to take over, through purchases or by force, their villages and homes—their native soil. By employing only Hebrew labour, the Zionists justify the shameful anti-Semitic slogan of 'each one to his own.' Also here, in Poland, Zionism pours oil on the fire of anti-Semitism. Didn't Isaac Grinbaum, the leader of the Polish Zionists, publicly state that there are a million too many Jews in Poland? There is no other choice, Pan Perlmuter argued, but to remain where we are and defend our lives and hard-won positions. We have to tie in our effort with the struggle of the Polish peasants, workers and intelligentsia for a better Poland. The working class learned its lesson from the German debacle—the rise of Hitler and Nazism. Now Communists, Socialists, and Democrats are uniting everywhere in a People's Front to bar the way for Fascism in Europe. And to the east is the Soviet Union, with its mighty Red Army that will ultimately crush the Nazi hydra. Thus, the fate of the Jews is inseparable from the fate of Europe; we must put our future on the card of the Social Revolution.

"And what if this card fails?" Nohum interrupted the teacher.

"This card will not fail," Pan Perlmuter answered. "There may be zigzags, defeats and retreats in the struggle, but all of Europe must proceed towards Socialism. The Jewish problem will then wither away, as in the Soviet Union. There, Jews are free to work on the land, in factories, in institutions of higher learning, and in the army. There, Jews may also chose either to assimilate or to develop, with government support, their own culture, in Yiddish."

Pan Perlmuter concluded his long political statement and fell silent. The children, too, remained quiet, their eyes and hearts lit with a vision of a better, more just world.

Chapter 16
THE PROTEST-STRIKE

The epidemic of anti-Semitism that engulfed all of Poland did not pass over the city of Otwock and the other resort towns along the Warsaw-Otwock railway line. Because of the abundance of pine trees and the golden, crisp sand in the open areas, these places were considered beneficial for the sick and healthy alike. During the summer, thousands of vacationers from Warsaw came here to enjoy the fresh air and the pleasant surroundings. In the early thirties, an electric train was installed along the line, and it took only about a half an hour to travel to or from Warsaw.

This whole area was heavily populated by Jews. They owned many villas, hotels, and boarding houses; they were also most of the patrons in the hotels and renters of the cottages. In addition, thousands of Jewish artisans, storekeepers, and vendors, as well as hotel workers, made their living from this vast summer resort industry.

This state of affairs drew the ire of many anti-Semites in the capital. Articles and caricatures often appeared in Warsaw newspapers decrying the "Judaisation" of the Warsaw-Otwock line. With the increase of anti-Semitism in the middle of the 1930's, physical attacks on Jews began also here, in Otwock, especially on the outskirts of the city.

Suddenly, a bomb exploded in the middle of the night, at the entrance to the bazaar where the Jewish quarter began. Although nobody was harmed, the explosion threw the Jewish population into panic. The representatives of the Jewish political parties began to discuss the establishment of a Jewish defence group that would keep watch and, if needed, defend the area.

At the same time, in March 1936, the Central Council of Jewish Workers' Unions, under the patronage of the Jewish Socialist Party, the "Bund," with the support of the Communists and leftist Zionists, proclaimed a general half-day protest-strike against the rising anti-Semitism in the country. In Jewish quarters all over Poland, Workers' Unions, party organizations, and youth leagues prepared feverishly for that day. The aim was to draw into action the broad Jewish masses—the petty merchants, artisans, and even the religious. All Jewish stores and enterprises were to be closed on the day of the protest-strike from morning until noon. Legal or illegal mass-meetings were planned for that morning in many towns and cities. Efforts were also made to have a delegate of the Polish Socialist Party at these gatherings, to show their support and solidarity for the Jews. Several days before the planned protest-strike, Moshe Gelman called Nohum aside during the long recess and said:

"Boy, can you keep a secret?"

"Let's hear it," Nohum was intrigued.

"You probably heard about the general protest-strike that will be held by the end of the week. Shouldn't we, too, do something here, in school? It would be a pity to sit in the classroom on such a day."

The bell rang and everyone began to hurry into the classrooms. Moshe tapped Nohum on the shoulder and said: "Today, at four o'clock at my house. We'll think up something. For sure?"

"Four o'clock, for sure!" Nohum answered.

Moshe was a head taller than Nohum, strong and broad-shouldered, with short, pitch black hair over his forehead. Since the ruffian, Leibel Davidowicz, had been thrown out of school at year's end in grade five, Moshe Gelman was considered the strongest in class. However, he was no cynic like Leibel and did not impose his rule over others.

Moshe's parents were fishmongers and his brothers pushed carts with fruit and vegetables in the bazaar. Moshe himself was sometimes absent from school, selling herring and tiny smoked fish at the market place. On the way home, his classmates would see him wearing a seller's apron and calling aloud: "Schmaltz herring, cucumbers, smoked fish! Here, here, cheap and tasty!"

Moshe wasn't at all embarrassed in front of his school friends. From childhood on, he was taught that to be poor is no shame, and to earn a few zlotys was honourable.

Lately, Nohum had befriended Moshe and began to like him more and more. In spite of his outer crudeness, Moshe possessed inner warmth, steadfastness of character, and loyalty to his friends.

"I dislike dessert-eaters and book-worms," Moshe used to say.

But despite Nohum's intellectual inclinations, Moshe did not consider him one of these despised species; he loved him like a younger brother and confided in him all his secrets.

At the agreed time, Nohum walked over to Moshe's place in a lane across the railway ramp. There he was greeted by two other classmates, Komar and Marek, both older boys who carried weight in all class matters. Moshe opened the meeting with a report on the preparations for the protest-strike all over the city. All stores and shops would be shut from morning till noon. Special ushers would be dispatched all over to see that everyone complied. A large unauthorized protest-meeting would be held at noon in the House of Study on Merchant Street. Moshe concluded by asking, "And us, will we sit in class and study on such a day?"

One by one the boys began to voice their proposals of what could be done at school. At the kitchen stove in the corner of the room, Moshe's mother, a husky market woman, was preparing supper for the family. She treated the boys with a plate of homebaked cookies and urged them on: "Think, children, think! Maybe you'll think up something to get rid of the enemies of Israel, may the earth swallow them."

After discussing all kinds of propositions, the boys unanimously agreed to organize on the morning of the protest-strike a march out of school by the whole grade seven. After leaving school, they will hold a brief meeting of their own and then proceed to the House of Study for the general meeting. Meanwhile, the four initiators were to convince and prepare the rest of the class for this daring action. They would leave during the first or second recess, Moshe and Nohum at the head, with Komar and Marek at the end, to make sure that nobody remained in the room.

On the morning of the strike, Nohum left for school as usual. On the way, along Bazaar Street, he noticed small groups of workers hurrying from place to place, reminding the shopkeepers not to open their stores. In the classroom, Moshe Gelman reproached Nohum:

"You are late, dessert-eater! I have been working already for half an hour with the bunch. It's fine. Everybody will follow us, right on the first recess." During the first session, Nohum and his comrades kept on sending messages all over the class.

"Leaving the first recess!"

"Nobody to remain in class!"

"All for one, and one for all!"

The bell rang and the teacher left, but nobody dared to move from his place. Moshe Gelman ran forward to the teacher's desk and thundered:

"Now, colleagues, it's time to act! All as one after me!"

Nohum followed him and after them all the boys and girls of grade seven, each one with his coat and schoolbag in hand. They ran wildly down the wooden stairs, thumping their feet and pushing one another. Doors opened and younger children looked on in amazement, a few of them joining the runners on the spur of the moment. Outside the school gate they stopped to see if they were followed. But neither a teacher nor the school director was seen.

"Is everybody here?" Moshe Gelman inquired.

"Only Pinkus remained in class," Komar reported. "He refused to move. We had to leave him."

"Such a traitor! Such a coward!" many children called with indignation.

"Let's move!" Moshe Gelman commanded. "The big one, our director, may come down and force us back. To the grove behind the large bakery!"

Excited and noisy, they marched along Karczew Street towards the white building of the bakery. Behind it was a sparsely wooded area where young people used to stroll on summer evenings. There Moshe Gelman stood up on top of a rock and began to speak: "Comrades and colleagues! Our leaving school is not a frivolous act or a usual outing. It's a bold demonstration, and it may carry serious consequences for each of us. Yet we are all here, the whole grade seven, with the exception of one coward and scab, in order to participate in the great protest manifestation against anti-Semitism and racial discrimination." "Hurray! Hurray!" the children cheered on Moshe.

"If anyone regrets leaving school," Moshe continued, "if anyone is willing to return, to join Pinkus—let him do it, he's free to go."

"Away with Pinkus! Away with traitors!" all responded.

Now Nohum replaced Moshe on top of the boulder. He waited a while until all quietened and began:

"Do you know why we, school children, undertook this action? Because in Przytyk innocent Jewish children were beaten and mistreated. With them, with the Jewish children, we solidarize." "Damn right! We do!" the whole group agreed.

Nohum continued: "Moshe has already explained that our leaving school may cause serious consequences. Pan Szymanski will surely try to find out who was behind this action. Therefore, let's now lift our right arms and solemnly swear that nobody will squeal. If we deserve to be punished, let them punish the whole class. All for one, and one for all, remember!" "We promise! We swear!" all called, lifting their right arms.

"And now," Nohum concluded, "we will all return to town to take part in the protest meeting at the synagogue."

Again the whole group proceeded along Karczew Street back into the city. Midway, before the market place, they turned to stop at the city's post office. There Nohum entered the telephone booth and asked with a changed voice for the director of School Number Four. Soon Nohum heard Pan Szymanski's distinguished voice, "Hello, who is it?" "Pan Director," Nohum yelled into the mouthpiece, "here speaks a representative of grade seven. We would like to explain why we all left school this morning. Today is a protest day against anti-Semitism and racial discrimination, and we felt that it's our duty to participate in it, in unity with all our brothers and sisters." "You are children!" exclaimed Pan Szymanski, "It's not for you to get involved in politics!"

"Pan Director," Nohum replied, "we stick up for the pogromed Jewish children of Przytyk. We stand up and protest for their sake!" Pan Szymanski hung up the receiver.

Now the class split into several groups, so as not to draw attention of the police and plainclothesmen around. They proceeded along the broad, open avenue overlooking the two railway tunnels and the station. From there, they cut through the bazaar toward Merchant Street. On the way, in the bazaar, they noticed the quietly controlled activity of the protest organizers. In twos and threes, they hurried to the few open stalls to remind the owners that it's high time to close business and leave for the synagogue. On Merchant Street, people were streaming from nearby streets and lanes towards the large House of Study. The doors as well as the windows of the synagogue were wide open and people flocked into them without stopping.

Not being able to receive a permit to hold the meeting in the open, the organizers of the protest day decided to seize the House of Study and hold the meeting there. Before Pinhas, the Shames, and the few Torah students that remained in the synagogue after the morning service could grasp what was happening, the synagogue was overflowing with people. Young men and women and middle-aged workers arrived from the nearby shops and stores in their workclothes, with or without caps or head coverings. They stood on the window sills, on the benches and tables; they filled the women's galleries and crowded around the almemor and the Holy Ark. In a short while, the large synagogue was filled with people, all waiting for the leaders to begin.

On the platform in the middle of the synagogue, the leaders of the different parties which had organized the protest were present. Among them was one tall Pole with a rounded, yellowish mustache—a delegate from the Polish Socialist Party. The stairs on both sides of the almemor were crowded by a host of party aides and members of their defence groups, ready for any eventuality.

Somebody banged his hand on the table to announce that the meeting had begun. Out of the group on the platform, Isidore, from the Workers' Union, came forward. Without a head-covering, in a dark, silken blouse halfways buttoned to the right side of his chest and belted with a silken belt, he stood for a while silently, waiting for complete silence. With dark, shining hair parted on the side, and a face sunken and bloodless, he looked like a recluse, a holy man from a monastery.

Isidore began in a low, dignified voice:

"Brothers and sisters, Jews from all walks of life! In the name of the United Committee Against Anti-Semitism and Racial Discrimination in our city, I open today's Protest Meeting." He then proceeded to describe the plight of the Jewish working man, petty artisan, and merchants whose meager positions were being assaulted through heavy taxation, economic boycott, and even pogroms." " All this is done to make us panic and leave the land. But this will not happen! As in time of the tzarist reactionaries, we will defend our life and honour, and we will prevail!" As he concluded, to the applause of the assembled, Isidore recalled in his memory the year 1905, when he, in his early twenties, participated in the uprising against the tzar on the streets of his hometown, Bialystok.

Now the turn came for comrade Nuske, the esteemed theoretician of the revolutionary movement in town. A bald, middle-aged man in a dark overcoat, he looked like any of the town's proprietors or storekeepers. Although not an active Communist Party member, Nuske was admired both by his comrades and opponents for his polite attitude to everyone, his sane judgements in everyday matters of the Workers' Union, and for his broad and thorough knowledge of all facets of Marxism and its various interpretations and commentaries. He was an old bachelor, a bookbinder by trade, and devoted all his free time and energy to the enlightenment of Jewish workers. He chaired and often lectured at cultural and political assemblies and celebrations at the Workers' Union.

Comrade Nuske began by setting the struggle against anti-Semitism in the broader framework of the current world situation. Not only are the three and a half million Polish Jews threatened, but the whole European civilization is at risk because of the rise of Fascism in Germany and elsewhere. "And what is Fascism?" he asked rhetorically. "It is an outgrowth of Capitalism in its decadent and degenerative stage. The pauperized mass of the petty bourgeoisie and the linchpins of monopolistic capital joined to bring forth Nazism—a bloodthirsty monster that will crush the workers' movement and all freedom-loving nations of Europe. When this Fascist hydra grows strong, it will begin a crusade against the Soviet Union, and thus, plunge Europe into a new war.

In this light, we should see the importance of the People's Front that unites workers, peasants, and the intelligentsia to halt the march of Fascism in Europe. This unity must be realized now and everywhere, with or without the consent of the myopic leaders." Comrade Nuske stopped a while, to take a sip of water from a glass somebody put before him, and continued in a low, broken voice:

"And we Jews, our situation is more precarious, our lives are more endangered because of our weakness and backwardness. But is there another way for us except to defend ourselves, to tie in our struggle with the one of the Polish proletariat and working people? No other road exists and on it we will persist until the bells of freedom will ring victoriously in our land and all over Europe." Nuske concluded his oration, and thunderous applause filled the House of Study.

The turn came for Moshe Richter, the leader of the left wing branch of the Poalei Zion. Moshe Richter grew up on Swiderska Street among the poorest of the poor. Both he and his brother Leibush were shoemakers. However, while Leibush chose to be a fiery Communist—already twice arrested for illegal activities—

Moshe became a Zionist, leader of the Poalei Zion party in town. He was an autodidact, well-versed in the writings of Borochov and Syrkin, and in addition, an excellent orator. Modest and gentle by nature, he was respected by the youth of the Jewish quarter, whatever their ideological attachment. Now he stood on the almemor, tall and serious, his long face tense and tauted upwards.

"Brother Jews," he began quietly, then quoted the Hebrew verse from the Passover Haggadah. 'In every generation our enemies rise to obliterate us.' For nearly two thousand years we have bled in different arenas of history. We are the scapegoat of all social systems, from monarchies in the dark ages of feudalism to the bourgeois-democratic republics of our century. The mass murders of the medieval crusaders were followed by the fires of the Spanish Inquisition; the pogroms during the Black Death epidemic by the blood libels and expulsions; and the Chmielnitski massacres by tzarist pogroms and persecutions. And now, in the midst of the twentieth century, we are witnessing a new resurgence of hatred and oppression—the rise of Nazism in Germany and the spread of anti-Semitism here, in Poland.

"Brothers and sisters! The time of passive sanctification of God's name is over! Jewish lives are no more free for all to take, not here and not in the Land of Israel! There the halutzim, the pioneers and guardsmen, the underground Jewish army—the Haganah—are defending Jewish settlements and cities from the Arab attackers and the British occupiers."

Moshe Richter stopped for a while to catch his breath and then continued to expand on the situation in Poland, after the rise of Nazism in neighbouring Germany. "According to logic," he argued, "Poland should be now completely free of anti-Semitism. Poland's independence is in great jeopardy: sooner or later Poland may be overrun by the armoured hordes of Germany. Instead of uniting all segments of the population to face this mortal danger, what does the government do? They divide the Polish and Jewish citizens, they incite the masses against Jewish artisans and merchants, market vendors and paupers. There's no logic is this policy except that it is guided by sheer and blind Jew-hatred. Don't give up, brother Jews!" Moshe Richter concluded. "Be united and strong in these times of trial! Bear proudly the name 'Jew'! Do not despair and lose hope of redemption! A time will come when Hitler and his minions will rot in the ground, and over the streets

91

of Tel Aviv and Jerusalem the blue-white flag will flutter, the flag of a free and independent Jewish state in Eretz Israel."

Tears glistened in his eyes when Moshe Richter finished his oration to the applause and cheers of all assembled. Then the last word was given to comrade Shalowski, the delegate of the Polish Socialist Party. After the long and lofty orations of his predecessors, his message was simple and concise: the Polish working class will join the struggle against anti-Semitism and the present reactionary regime.

Comrade Isidore, the chairman of the meeting, came forward and, after reading the text of the protest resolution that was unanimously accepted, announced that the meeting was over. All as one rose and joined in the singing of the Internationale.

As the crowd left, policemen outside the synagogue dispersed the people with rubber batons and made several arrests.

Next morning, the pupils of grade seven arrived in school as if nothing had happened. Pan Szymanski, who gave the first lesson in geography, entered the class without his cheerful 'good morning'. His face was clouded and strained and the children could see that he forced himself to conduct the lesson as usual. They sat fearfully in their seats, awaiting what will come next. Finally, at the end of the lesson, Pan Szymanski exploded:

"What happened to all of you yesterday? Are you a gang of street kids or pupils in a Polish school?! Never in my life have I witnessed such a behaviour: to walk out of school in the middle of sessions? Who talked you into this? Are you aware of the consequences that may follow?" A deadly silence fell over the class. The faces of the children paled, they lowered their eyes, not to face the director's angry looks. Suddenly, Estusia Eiger, the tiniest girl in class, stood up and declared:

"Pan Director! We left school because we wanted to participate in the Protest Day against anti-Semitism, in solidarity with children of Przytyk, who suffered, along with grown-ups, in the excesses."

"Who taught you this?!" Pan Szymanski exclaimed, standing up from his chair. "It's not from your head, Estusia. I heard the same words yesterday over the phone from an elderly person..." The bell rang and the director left the class without a word.

Soon the investigations began. One by one the students were called into the director's office for questioning. Pan Szymanski tried hard to squeeze out the names of the organizers of the strike, but nobody disclosed anything. The children implored each other to be courageous and strong. Some came out with tears in their eyes, but none of them broke the solidarity vow. In the end, Pan Szymanski got tired of the useless investigation and called an evening meeting of all grade seven parents. There he reproached them for allowing their children to be drawn into dubious political actions. He then announced that, on the advice of the Regional School Inspector, the grade seven pupils would be allowed to graduate, but with a lowered mark in conduct. However, should a similar incident occur, anyone involved in it would certainly be expelled. Relieved that nobody was really punished, the parents hurried to their homes to bring the good news to the children.

The only one who really suffered from the whole affair was the religion teacher, Pan Perlmuter. Although he had no hand in the action—he was away in Warsaw on that day—Pan Szymanski saw him as the instigator. Soon afterwards, he received permission to replace Pan Perlmuter with another religion teacher from the seminary in Warsaw. On the last lesson, Pan Perlmuter read before the class "The Three Gifts" by I.L. Peretz—a gem of a story about Jewish suffering and martyrdom. During the lunch break, all the children accompanied him to the gate. Pressing his hands and begging for his inscriptions in their memento booklets, they all assured him:

"We'll never forget you, Pan Perlmuter! You'll always be remembered by us!"

"I won't forget you, too," Pan Perlmuter promised as he patted their heads and shoulders lovingly. He then tore himself away from them and left for the train to Warsaw.

The other person who suffered as a result of the event was Pinkus, who had remained in class when all the others left. His classmates could not forgive his betrayal and they pestered and annoyed him till the end of the year.

Chapter 17
IN THE WORKERS' UNION

During the winter, Moshe-Avrohom spent most of the day in his restored workshop, on the upper floor, trying to get some additional income from his boot-stitching trade. His wife remained downstairs, in the restaurant, assisted by Nohum, after his return from school. During the day, only a few customers came in for a quick snack or a hot bowl of soup. However, in the evening, some of the street people gathered to spend their leisure hours at card and domino games.

The games were held in the back room of the restaurant. The players sat around tables surrounded by onlookers and advisers who shared in the excitement of the play. The chief player was Yudel the Lame, a wandering railway singer and mendicant. He had a shaven head, with a short, red beard and wore a frayed uniform and hat of a railway worker. In this outfit, he travelled in passenger trains all over the country, singing pensive Polish songs and collecting donations afterwards. After spending several weeks on the road, he would return home to spend his days and evenings in the beer-halls and restaurants. Passionately involved in the game, he used to sing his Polish travel songs, tapping rhythmically on the floor with his wooden leg.

During the slow winter season, these games were a source of income, and Moshe-Avrohom had to allow them. From time to time, during the long evening, the gamblers ordered from the buffet something to eat or drink. In addition, the players had to pay a fee of five groschen for a domino game and ten groschen for a round of cards. Over the evening, these payments, collected by Nohum, amounted to an income of several zlotys. Thus, Nohum had to spend his evening in the smoke-filled and noisy back room among the gamblers and street people.

Nohum, tucked at a table in a corner, paid little attention to the noisy and obscene chatter of the players. Now in grade seven, his horizon widened and he was absorbed in his readings of prose and poetry, history and social issues. From time to time he had to return to the reality around him, in order to collect the fees from the gamblers. Sometimes the gambling continued till past midnight, and Nohum rose next morning, drowsy and red-eyed. Itte pitied him and complained to her husband that the boy is being ruined by these late night sessions. Moshe-Avrohom was silent and adamant; there was no other way that the business could survive during these hard months. He himself had to attend at night the few customers that showed up in the front room of the restaurant, while his wife, who was becoming weaker with every year, needed to rest in the evening, after her long day in the kitchen. Besides, it was not proper for a woman to spend long hours among the coarse card players and street people. There was no choice—Nohum had to watch over the gambling room during the long winter evenings.

One night, it was late in March, the restaurant was suddenly raided by policemen. It was already past midnight, when the shut doors of the restaurant were opened and the policemen rushed straight into the back room. Nohum woke up from his drowsiness and saw the players running out through the back door into the courtyard, leaving the scattered cards and domino pieces on the tables. Some, however, did not manage to escape and had to remain in their seats until their names and addresses were noted down by the policemen. After letting them free, the two policemen returned to the front store to question the restaurateur and write a report.

For several days, Moshe-Avrohom walked around deeply troubled and distraught. To keep a gambling place was a serious offence; it could involve a court trial and a large fine. Finally, he succeeded, through intermediaries, in paying off the policemen so they did not proceed further in the matter. The gifts for the policemen and intermediaries fee amounted to a hundred and fifty zlotys, nearly all that remained from his savings of the summer season. Moreover, the gambling had, for the time being, to be stopped, and thus the restaurant's revenues shrank even more. Meanwhile, tax and utility bills had to be paid, as well as rent and payments for delivered merchandise.

Then, in one early spring afternoon, the wagon of the taxation office halted in front of the restaurant. A uniformed clerk with a leather briefcase entered and, without much ado, began to make an inventory of the restaurant's fixtures and furniture that could be taken away for the unpaid taxes. With the taxman came Henech the Scruf-head, the driver for the taxation office. A stout Jew with a simpleton's smile on his unshaven face, he stood silently, whip in hand, waiting for orders from his superior.

Henech was disliked by the town's people for his eagerness to serve the taxman's office. Some considered him not only the coachman, but an informer to the dreaded tax clerks. No wonder then that he earned the despicable name of Henech the Scruf-head.

Moshe-Avrohom stood beside the buffet, silent and helpless, while Itte clung to the table where the taxman sat, pleading with him to give them a respite. Her thin body trembled and tears flowed over her cheeks as she stammered in her broken Polish:

"Dear Pan, have pity on us! Give us a break! Summer is near, and we'll pay off everything, to the last zloty!"

Without saying a word, the clerk got up and pointed his finger to the square icebox in the corner beside the entrance door.

"For the time being," he mumbled, "we'll take only this. Maybe you'll pay off the rest."

Henech the Scruf-head, who stood unmoved beside the door, jumped from his place and flung the doors of the restaurant wide open. His young Polish assistant, who sat outside in the wagon, rushed in and both of them lifted the icebox and carried it through the door. Itte ran after them, grabbed at the edge of the box crying, "Don't take away my icebox! Summer is coming and where will I keep a bit of ice for the food? You are robbers! Without a bit of mercy!" Henech and his helper pushed her away and placed the icebox on the wagon. The taxman left, the coachmen climbed on the wagon, and away they went.

Soon after the tax execution, an even heavier blow came upon Moshe-Avrohom and his family—the eviction from the two-room apartment on the floor upstairs. During the winter, Moshe-Avrohom was behind in his monthly payments for the two locations he kept, and Itchele, the landlord, decided to take away from him one dwelling—the rooms upstairs. To convey this decision to Moshe-Avrohom fell upon Itchele's adopted son, Leibel. One could see that Leibel resented his task, but his uncle's word was a command that had to be obeyed.

"The uncle wants you to know," Leibel announced hesitantly, "that you have to vacate the rooms upstairs by the end of the month. He says, it's too much for you to hold on to two dwellings..."

In vain Moshe-Avrohom tried to argue with Leibel, and later with the landlord himself, that he'll soon get an interest-free loan and pay off the rent; Itchele got a court injunction which had to be obeyed.

In the evenings, so not to make a fuss, Moshe-Avrohom and Nohum took apart the household furniture and the sewing machines and dragged them downstairs into the back room of the restaurant. Thus Nohum and his family returned full circle back to the room where they lived years ago, when Nohum was a child and his father an owner of a boot-stitching shop.

As in the old days, the two beds were placed along the wall, up to the window into the courtyard. One sewing machine and a cutting table were squeezed in the corner at the window, beside the second bed. The wooden partition that ran from the stove to the courtyard door, where Moshe-Avrohom's wife used to do her cooking and baking, was taken apart to add more space to the one room amalgamation of family home, boot-stitching shop and kitchen, both for the household and the shrunken restaurant in the front.

Passover was near and Itte worked hard to bring the place in order for the holiday. The room was overcrowded with household possessions and workshop tools, with the five children and the two grown-ups filling the little space that remained. It was almost impossible to keep the children clean and groomed for the festive season. At the Passover table, Moshe-Avrohom recited aloud from the Haggadah in a subdued voice, aware of his own and his family's misery and tribulations. Nohum was even more upset and agitated. Everything in him cried against the bitter lot that had befallen them—the return, after all those years of effort and travail, to the same back room of his childhood, with its dank walls and sunless window. Unless you change the order of things as they are, he thought, the poor man is ordained to the pitiful life of an underling, no matter what he does and how hard he strives. But the laws of this order are not laws of nature, he argued to himself, they are man-made and could be changed or rearranged by the will of the people, by the force of their suffering and despair. He, Nohum, will never make peace with this unjust state of things; he'll continue to dream and to struggle for something better and higher than this underdog life of his and his family ...

In the afternoon on the second day of Passover, Nohum attended, for the first time, a youth meeting at the Workers' Union. He was taken there by Moshe Gelman who had been a member of the Union's Youth Section for some time. The Workers' Union was an amalgam of several small trade associations: needle and leather workers, painters, and carpenters—all dominated by the underground Communist Party of the city. Through these unions, the Party found a legal outlet both for trade union work, and for political and cultural activities among the Jewish population.

Every Friday night, open question-and-answer meetings were held at the Union's local at which the leaders of the movement discussed current political events or social problems raised by the audience. Various other activities and lectures were also held on different occasions, such as First of May assemblies, Sylvester nights, and anti-religious evenings. The Union was often harassed by the police, who were well aware of its structure and activities. From time to time, they raided the premises and sealed off the local. But the Union soon found another dwelling, changed its name or the composition of its Executive Committee, and continued its activities as before. Now the Workers' Union was at the far end of Swiderska Street, on an open, sandy stretch of land, dotted on its outskirts with fenced cottages and vegetable gardens.

The two rooms of the Union were full of young people, workers and journeymen from different shops and trades. Dressed in their Sabbath best, they congregated in groups, chatting together. Others sat on benches, absorbed in books or newspapers, or smoked cigarettes in a carefree manner. Somebody announced that the meeting was to begin and the several rows of benches were filled immediately. At the head table sat the Chairman of the Youth Section, Asher Silver, and at his side the secretary, Yosef Krulik. Asher was the youngest of three brothers, all of them heavily involved in the local Communist movement. The oldest one, Meir, a tall, stalwart man, was renowned for his daring acts of bravery in clashes with police during First of May demonstrations in his younger days. Later on, he had settled down and opened a sandal shop with several partners. Yet he remained a sympathizer and staunch supporter of the movement. Another of the brothers, Alter, was one of the suspects involved in the assassination of a provocateur. He had been forced to flee to France and from there, it was told, he went to Spain, to join the International Brigade of the Republican Army. Asher, the youngest of the brothers, was a slender, well-built man in his late twenties. On both sides of his mouth were deep creases and his short cut hair was stricken with grayness—visible signs of the treatment he had received during the two years spent in prison after his arrest at an illegal First of May demonstration.

Asher opened the meeting with a report of the activities of the Youth Section during the winter months, followed by an outline of the projected activities for the spring season. One of these was to be a 'Living Newspaper' that the Youth Section, in conjunction with the Cultural Committee of the Union, would be holding a week from now, on the last day of Passover. All comrades should make sure to attend and bring as many friends and sympathizers as they can.

A discussion began on the chairman's report. Pinie Cukerkop, a tall youngster with blond curly hair and a red-pimpled face, came up to the front and, stuttering from time to time, commended the Committee of the Youth Section for undertaking the forthcoming activity. "Only through such ventures," Pinie concluded, "will we broaden our base and bring more youngsters under the wings of our proletarian culture."

"Enough, Pinie!" some called out from the back benches.

"All the dumb like to speak a lot," somebody added.

The secretary of the Youth Section, comrade Yosef Krulik, who sat silently beside the chairman, asked for the floor. He was a short fellow with pudgy cheeks, tight-lipped and with a stern, almost angry look. Krulik explained that the 'Living Newspaper' is yet far from completion. The editors need more material—articles, book-reviews, poems, and humorous pieces. As time is short, everybody's cooperation and help is needed. "Who among you is willing to contribute some additional material?" asked Krulik. Moshe Gelman, who sat beside Nohum, suddenly got up and pointed at Nohum. "Here, my friend, is an excellent writer. His written assignments are the best in class..."

Asher got up from his seat and turned to Nohum.

"What is your name, comrade?"

"Nohum, Nohum Freidowicz..."

"Please rise, comrade Nohum," Asher insisted.

Nohum rose and blushed, as all the eyes of the assembled turned towards him.

"Will you write something for our newspaper?" Asher asked.

"Well, I'll try," Nohum answered hesitantly.

"Can you tell us about what you'll write?"

Nohum thought a while and said, "Something about the life of our youth."

"Excellent! It's exactly what we need!" Asher concluded with a broad smile.

Thus, on the last day of Passover, on a bright afternoon, Nohum and Moshe Gelman attended the reading of the 'Living Newspaper.' In the audience were the members of the Youth Section and their friends, some of the older comrades and activists of the Union, and even members of the leftist Zionist youth organizations. Both rooms of the Union were overflowing with people. At the head table was Little Leon, chief editor of the newspaper. Leon was a stout man of about thirty, with a full face, flat nose, and thick, sensitive lips. His head was adorned with thick, black bangs, and his eyes were sharp and penetrating. He came from a small town in eastern Poland, and had lived for some years in Warsaw, where he learned to be a good custom tailor. In spite of his involvement in both the legal and illegal work of the Movement, Leon found time for serious study in Marxism and the humanities. He spoke with controlled emotion, quoting without notes, from Marxist and European literature. In his free hours, late at night, he himself wrote short stories and playlets with a political content.

One by one, Little Leon introduced the participants in the 'Living Newspaper' to read their writings. These varied from serious editorials to short stories and poems, satires of political opponents or fiery declarations in support of the People's Front in France and in Spain. Nohum's time arrived, and Leon announced:

"Comrade Nohum Freidowicz will read an essay, 'We Want To Live.' Nohum came forth to the podium. Scared and pale-faced, he began to read his paper, his voice becoming stronger and more assured as he read. In short and succinct sentences, he described the feelings of his and his colleagues from the graduating class of the public school, and their fear that all doors to a productive and meaningful life were closed for them. How much ability as well as talent, he asked, are wasted and lost? How much energy and enthusiasm are nipped and smothered in these unfavourable conditions? Many young people try to forget their misery by attending dance halls or getting involved in alcoholism and in crime. The conscious proletarian youth is, therefore, the vanguard of all the young people in the country. They should not allow the young generation to sink into despair, to lose hope and vision of a better future, of a new and just social order—Nohum concluded to the applause of all. As soon as the readings were over, Moshe Gelman squeezed Nohum's hand in appreciation and said, "Boy, you were excellent! Short and good!" Little Leon also came over to shake hands with Nohum.

"You have ability, young man. You write from the heart."

Free and noisy groups formed as the audience left the premises on the way to their homes. Boys and girls walked arm in arm, commenting aloud on the content and the participants in the 'Living Newspaper.' Nohum and Moshe walked beside Little Leon, engaged in a friendly conversation. Leon was in high spirits. The cultural event he had prepared had been successful both in attendance and in content. In addition, he had gained a new and able pupil—Nohum Freidowicz.

Chapter 18
THE GRADUATION

It was the beginning of summer, before the end of the school year. The air in Nohum's classroom became hot and sticky and there was no eagerness to study, in class or at home. However, all grade seven students were aware of the threat hanging over their heads since the protest-strike in March. Pan Szymanski was still tense and agitated, ready to punish anyone for the slightest breach of discipline. However, the end of the school year was near, the students comforted themselves, then they will finally rid themselves of the whole routine in which they were constricted for so many years. But for the few remaining weeks, there was no choice but to continue with the studies, write compositions, mathematical exercises, and learn poems by heart.

The question of how to celebrate their graduation from public school was now heatedly discussed during and after the lessons. There was an established tradition that the graduating class travelled, under the supervision of several teachers, to faraway sites in Poland: the Tatry mountains, the port of Gdynia on the Baltic Sea, or the historical city of Cracow. Such excursions lasted several days, even a week.

However now, with the rise of anti-Semitism in the country, the parents as well as the school administration had serious misgivings about such an undertaking. The class had to settle for a one-day trip to nearby Warsaw. There they would view the presidential palace and then travel by boat on the Vistula to Wilanow, the residence of the last Polish king. The remaining funds, which the class had saved during the year, were to be used for a lavish graduation party on the last day of school.

On a sunny June morning, the whole class, led by Pani Pola and Pan Klar, left by train for Warsaw. All the students were neatly dressed—the boys in sport jackets or blouses with open collars; the girls in white blouses and dark skirts, all happy, high-spirited and talkative. In the midst of a circle of boys sat Pan Klar, recalling his adventurous summers among the Huculs, a tribe in the Tatry mountains. In another corner was Pani Pola, surrounded by a group of girls, all giggling and enjoying themselves. Nohum walked around in the coach sharing everyone's joy. "How good it is to be young," he thought, "to grow up in the midst of friends, boys and girls of your age."

Alone, at the window in the passage way, stood Dora, a tall, dark-haired girl with a gentle, sad smile on her lips. Since the beginning of the school year, Nohum had been attracted and had often daydreamed of her, never daring to let her know about his feelings. Here and there he had tried to talk to her during recess or on school outings, but Dora was always quiet and unresponsive. Now, as he stood in the corridor of the coach, Nohum was wondering again how he could approach her. As he lingered at the next window, Dora left and returned to her girlfriends in the compartment. The train reached the outskirts of Warsaw. From afar one could distinguish the contours of factory buildings, their tall chimneys puffing pillars of dark smoke into the air. Soon the train arrived in Praga, a suburb of Warsaw, on the eastern bank of the Vistula. The students got ready to disembark, anxious to begin this memorable visit to Poland's capital city.

From the Praga railway station, the group travelled by streetcar over the Vistula bridge to the nearby Zamek—the residence of Poland's rulers—the last kings, the tzar's governors, and now of President Moscicki. The various wings of the Zamek, spread along the shore of the Vistula, were an island of quiet and serenity at the edge of the great, bustling city. Here and there, gendarmes in colourful uniforms stood on guard at gates and entrances.

Through one of the sideways, the class entered the palace. Here they had to put on special soft slippers and began the long walk through the ornate halls and chambers, all filled with statues, mirrors, and paintings. Leading them was Pani Pola, who, it seemed, was familiar with the place from previous visits and excursions. With unabashed enthusiasm, she lingered in front of the heavily framed oil paintings by Matejko and other Polish masters who had immortalized in great works of art Poland's struggle for freedom and independence. On one of the canvases, King Jan Sobieski was leading his hussars towards Vienna to save Europe from the barbaric Turks; on others, knights in shining armour were fighting German Crusaders, Swedish intruders, or rebellious Cossacks. Pani Pola's eyes glistened and her voice trembled with emotion as she recalled these glorious pages of Poland's past.

After a brief rest on the stony stairs of the palace, the class boarded a steamer that would take them, upstream on the Vistula, to Wilanow. The boat glided slowly over the quiet surface of the river in the golden sunshine of the afternoon. Everyone was out on the deck, enjoying the breeze and viewing the landscape on both shores of the river. A small orchestra played popular dance music and some couples began dancing in the middle of the deck. Resting on benches, the students opened their lunch bags and started to eat.

As on the train, Nohum wandered over the deck, observing the passengers and admiring the changing view on the shores of the river.

"It's so beautiful here," Nohum suddenly heard a familiar voice say. He turned around and saw next to him, at the railing of the deck, Dora. Her short brownish hair was ruffled by the wind, her eyes were dreamy and the sad smile played, as always, on her lips. Nohum blushed and his heart began to beat faster. "Dora," he whispered and fell silent. For a while they both stood without uttering a word.

"What will you do after graduation?" Nohum finally asked.

"After graduation?" Dora wondered, "I'll probably work in my brother's tailoring atelier in Warsaw. Later on I may go to America."

"To America?" Nohum repeated in astonishment. "Don't you mind leaving everyone here?"

"Whom do I have here?" Dora replied. "My father is an invalid, can hardly go on working. And my mother, she has enough daughters without me... I'll go abroad, to my uncle in America."

Nohum moved closer to Dora. Quietly he took her hand and whispered as if to himself: "Dora, I love you..."

Several familiar girls suddenly approached and began giggling and teasing Nohum and Dora.

"See who is here! What a romantic pair."

Dora withdrew her hand and left without saying another word.

The steamer arrived to Wilanow. Sunburned and happy, the students entered the gates of the palace which stood amidst a thick pine and oak forest. The royal residence was built in neo-classical style by Polish craftsmen and imported Italian artists. The exterior was adorned with white marble columns, small statues, and elaborate carvings. Two symmetrical towers and gables rose on both flanks of the ornate entrance and added majesty and grandeur to the historic mansion.

After walking for a while through the glittering halls and chambers, the students ventured into the surrounding woodland, calling each other from afar, or circling, by joining hands, the thick ancient pine trees and oaks. Nohum looked for Dora, but she made an effort to avoid him and walked around all the time with her girlfriends.

Soon the class boarded the steamer again and returned to Warsaw. Tired from the day long walking and touring, the graduating class arrived home in the evening, filled with impressions of a long and memorable day.

After the excursion, the class began to prepare for the graduation party. Boys ventured after school hours into the groves for greenery and girls fashioned paper festoons to decorate the walls and ceiling of the hall where the party was to be held. Others busied themselves and involved their mothers with baking cakes and cookies or preparing home-made ice cream.

On the last day of school, after receiving their report cards, the students were dismissed early, to prepare themselves for the evening. They were excited and happy, compared marks and congratulated one another on their achievements. Some girls ran from classmate to classmate, asking them to sign their colourful memento booklets. Others took leave from their teachers, wishing them a happy summer vacation. By noontime, the school premises were empty and quiet.

Early in the evening, the grade seven pupils returned for their celebration. In the middle of the hall, a long table, covered with white tablecloths, was set with all kinds of sweets and soft drinks. The colourful paper-chains fluttered in the bright light of the hall and the green branches on the walls added shade and colour to the festive surroundings. The pupils and teachers, dressed up for the occasion, took their seats around the table. Among them was the school director, Pan Szymanski, and his wife, now both cheerful and friendly.

Pan Szymanski opened the evening with a short talk on the significance of the occasion. He assured his pupils that he forgave them their misbehaviour during the year and he wished them well after leaving school. However, he appealed to them to remain loyal citizens of the Fatherland whose earth nourishes all her sons and daughters, irrespective of race and religion.

Moshe Gelman, who sat beside Nohum, could not restrain himself and grumbled: "Hollow wishes. Deeds, not words, are needed!"

Pani Szymanska, who sat across the table, caught Moshe's words and replied softly: "The world is not ideal, Moses. There will never be absolute equality and justice. All we can do is help each other wherever possible."

"I don't mean this," Moshe did not let up. "Never mind alms and philanthropy. Change, radical solutions are needed!"

Afraid that the discussion will get out of hand, Nohum kicked Moshe's leg under the table to let him know that it's time to leave the subject.

"I whistle on all of them!" Moshe continued defiantly. "My report card is at home, and he can do nothing to me now."

The girls brought saucers with ice cream and chunks of fancy cake, and everyone began to eat. Popular dance tunes were played on the record player and some of the bolder boys asked a few girls to dance. Others split in groups and began all kinds of games that test the memory and intelligence of the participants.

Nohum walked around, spending some time with each group and sharing their enjoyment. From his childhood he had loved festivities, like those on Purim and Simchat Torah in the synagogue, when everyone, young and old, was elevated out of grey reality into a realm of joy. Although Dora avoided him all the evening, he did not mind it any more. Since the excursion to Warsaw, he had decided to let her go her own way and follow her no more.

At the open window in the corner of the hall, he noticed Franka, Dora's girlfriend, who had sat down to rest a while after all the work and preparations for the party.

"The hostess is tired, it looks," Nohum said jokingly.

"Sit down, Nohum," Franka said with a sincere smile. Nohum moved over and sat beside her. "Franka is beautiful, and smart as well," he thought, "and he, Nohum, never noticed it."

For the whole year his desk was behind Franka's, but he continued to look over her shoulders at Dora's pale face with its sad smile. Now he noticed how Franka blossomed, as if overnight, from the chubby girl who had sat in front of him, into this charming young woman. Her clear, round face looked both serious and playful, her eyes were large and deep and the lips full and passionate. The white collared summer dress she wore complimented her dark, braided hair and a white belt accentuated her waist and slightly rounded breasts.

"You look beautiful tonight, Franka," Nohum said boldly.

"Thank you for the compliment," Franka answered. "You must have said it tonight to a lot of girls..."

"No, you are the first one," Nohum said and blushed.

Nohum moved over closed and laid his hand on Franka's shoulder, touching her soft braids with delight. He never before felt so happy, and he spent the rest of the evening at Franka's side.

A few days after the graduation party, most of the grade seven pupils gathered in a shop on Bazaar Street, in the courtyard of one of the well-to-do students. After so many years of studying and socializing, it was hard for them to accept that, from now on, everyone would go his own way. An idea of organizing a club of graduates was raised, in order to meet and be in touch from time to time. Now they sat in the dimly lit shop among barrels and piles of wood, wondering aloud what could be done. Moshe Gelman climbed a pile of lumber and began preaching:

"Friends and colleagues! Let's organize and continue our self-education, instead of wasting time in the dance halls."

Nobody paid attention to his words; all talked and argued at the same time.

"To hell with you! Let me finish!" Moshe thundered.

"Crawl down, red yokel! Enough of you!" other defied him.

Exhausted and hoarse from trying to quieten the group, Nohum realized that nothing will be achieved at this meeting. Without the framework of the school, there was now no common bond to hold them together. A new idea sparked in his mind. He climbed the top of a barrel and called over the heads of all: "Dear colleagues! Listen! I have a new idea to which everybody will agree!" Slowly the classmates quietened down, eager to hear Nohum's proposal. Nohum continued:

"Let's give up the idea of a club of graduates. Let everyone continue on his own in whatever group or organization he wishes to belong. But, I propose, that in five years from now, on the day of our graduation, all of us should meet to celebrate our anniversary and share our experiences of all these years. Let's solemnly promise that wherever we'll be, we'll do everything possible to meet and renew the bonds of our comradeship, here in Otwock."

"Hurray! Hurray," all called. "A wonderful proposal! Only Nohum can come up with such an idea!"

"Let's lift up our right hand in an oath," somebody suggested. The whole shop was hushed as the assembled youngsters stood up, in silence, with uplifted hands.

On the way home, Nohum wondered how he got the idea of meeting five years from now. Would his classmates remember the vow and be willing or able to realize it? And where would he, and all of them, be in 1941, just five short years from now?

Chapter 19
ON THE THRESHOLD OF LIFE

The first few days after leaving school, Nohum felt uneasy, not knowing what to do and how to begin his new life. It was midsummer and both his father and mother were occupied in the one-room restaurant from morning till late at night. Strained and restless, Nohum left the restaurant after breakfast to wander along Swiderska Street. Although he had grown up here and was familiar with every nook and corner, he always found something new to observe.

A block away from his home was Gorna Street that led along courtyards and villas, to the Swider River. Down on Gorna lay Pinai's villa, a spacious area of luscious grass and shady trees, with a few wooden houses in their midst. There he could lie on the grass, resting, reading and daydreaming as much as his heart desired. Then Nohum remembered that he had promised to put the library at the Worker's Union in order. He decided to spend his day there.

He continued along Swiderska Street. Across from the tall dilapidated brick apartment house on the corner was a chain of attached one storey houses, half sunken in the ground. From the open doors and windows he heard the shrill voices of women, together with the buzzing of sewing machines and the tapping of cobblers' hammers. On a low stool in front of a door sat the widow Alte-Naome, bathing her frail body in the morning sun. Since her younger son, Leibushel, had been arrested after the protest-meeting, her life seemed to be caving in. All her attention she now focused on her older son, Moshe, who, thanks to the One Above, had turned out to be a Zionist. Still better than one of these hunted 'reds'. Through the window Nohum noticed her son Moshe bent over his shoemaker's workbench and he recalled the protest-meeting in the House of Study where Moshe foretold that the blue-white flag of a Jewish State would flutter over the streets of Jerusalem and Tel-Aviv. "Will the prophecy of this shoemaker come true?" Nohum asked himself. He remembered his own sister, Shaindel, still away from home on Hachsharah, still awaiting the certificate that would enable her to enter Palestine. "All of them want to leave, for Palestine, America or elsewhere. Who will remain here?" Nohum wondered. He, however, had committed himself to remain, to stay put with those who will endure the social upheaval that was brewing and that would eventually create a new reality...

Nohum continued along the uneven sidewalk of Swiderska Street. In Elie the Blacksmith's open courtyard he noticed the flying sparks from the open doors of the smithy. Across the street, from Berish Bursztyn's bakery chimney, strings of smoke rose into the clear sky. Inside the sunken homes further on, bearded Jews in open shirts, with fringed undergarments beneath, were busy laundering linen. Next door, carpenters worked their sharp planes over long wooden boards. Swiderska Street was in the midst of its daily sweat and toil to earn its livelihood. Further on, at the corner of Staszica Street, Nohum entered the large, sparsely wooded courtyard where the communal institutions—the Talmud Torah and the Bikkur Holim Society—were housed. The Talmud Torah was attended mainly by children of the poor, who could not afford to send them to a private Heder. From the open windows of the classrooms came the children's choral recitation of psalmic verses from the morning prayers:

> Happy are those
> Who dwell in Thy house;
> They will praise Thee
> For ever and ever.

Behind the Talmud Torah building, Nohum noticed a circle of women and children surrounding Shmelke the Lithuanian and his son, Vove. Shmelke, tall and thin, had a short fiery-red beard and wild eyes in his haggard waxen face. Panting and sweating, he lashed his son Vove with a leather strap. "I'll tear you by the roots! I'll mortify you!" Shmelke screamed in his Lithuanian-Yiddish dialect.

Shmelke lived with his wife and son in a rundown cottage on the far end of the courtyard. Nobody knew from where they came

110

and why he, a Lithuanian, chose to dwell among Polish Jews. Shmelke was a dire pauper who never tried to work for a living. This he left to his wife who made a very small amount from washing linen in well-to-do houses. Usually, such a washing lasted several days and she ate at her place of work and was able to bring home some food as well as a few zlotys. Still, the family often went hungry and survived only because of occasional assistance of some good-hearted neighbours. Embittered by this kind of life, Shmelke often unloaded his anger upon his wife and son.

"Darkness, poverty, need all around," Nohum thought. "All this will have to be restructured, built anew, when the social revolution comes...There will be lots to do..."

Nohum proceeded further, to where the street ended into an open sandy tract. To the right, enclosed in a wooden fence, was the Marpeh Sanatorium for those stricken with consumption. Some of the patients sauntered in the narrow, shaded lanes, others rested on folding beds and lawn chairs in the open verandas. "For them," Nohum thought, "all is over. Slowly they spit out their lungs and disappear silently from life's stage. Their misfortune is also a result of social evils—malnutrition, unsanitary dwellings and overwork. All evils of society lead to the same source—the corrupt system of private ownership. You change this order and everything will fall into place—the social body will recover from all its ills and pains."

Nohum trudged over the soft, sandy ground towards the local of the Worker's Union. The place was closed during the day; its organizers and officers were all working-men, busy during the day in their shops. Nohum entered the yard, opened one of the windows from the outside, and climbed in.

Both rooms of the local were empty. The sun flooded through the uncurtained window-panes and coloured the bare walls in all shades of gold and red. On one of the walls hung a black-and-white portrait of Karl Marx in an old dust-covered frame. His white beard shimmered in the sunlight, and his eyes, under the wide forehead, were deep with insight and wisdom.

"The prophet of our time," Nohum thought, "the master-healer and miracle-worker who will drive out all evil spirits of this world."

111

In the second room stood an old bookcase with the Union's book collection. Because of the various movings the Union had to undergo due to police harassment, the library was in constant disarray. Books were placed on the shelves haphazardly, in no order. Some were lying flat, one top of another, others were torn and falling apart. The official librarian, Moshe Manchuria—so-called because of his bony, Mongolian face—had no time or patience to sort out the books and had appealed to the members of the Youth Section to give him a hand. Nohum was the only one who had volunteered and helped him out on several occasions.

Nohum rolled up his sleeves and began the work. He examined each book, dusted it and put it on the proper shelf according to its literary genre. Here were Yiddish translations of the great Russian and Western masters; novels by Maxim Gorki, Sholokhov and other contemporary Soviet writers; numerous old Yiddish periodicals, pamphlets and brochures—all jumbled and intermixed. As he picked up each book and dusted it, Nohum read the title page and here and there looked inside. Sometimes he became intrigued and read whole paragraphs or pages at random. A variety of protagonists, from different epochs welcomed him from these yellowing pages; tragic events, wars and battles echoed in them; man's struggle with nature and with himself—all these were recalled and reflected in those pages. In the outdated political pamphlets one could still feel the passionate heat of discussions and polemics between the revolutionary movement and its adversaries of all sorts. Reports of expeditions to Brobidzhan—in the Far East of Soviet Russia—told of a Jewish Autonomous Region to be built there.

Hungry for knowledge and understanding, Nohum swallowed all this until his eyes were strained and his head became dizzy. To catch his breath, he now switched to poetry books where the lines were sparse and more readable. Here were the proletarian Yiddish poets of the American sweatshop—Morris Rosenfeld, Edelstadt, Winchevski or the folksy Abraham Reisen. Afterwards came the thin, soft-cover collections of the contemporary revolutionary Yiddish poets in Poland—Moshe Shulshtein, Bunem Heller and others. Their poems about strikes, demonstrations or the suffering of the impoverished and unemployed, were permeated with revolutionary fervour that ignited Nohum's heart and imagination.

It was already late afternoon when Nohum's head became heavy from too much reading and he began to feel hungry. He decided that it was enough for the day, dusted his shirt and pants, and left, again through the window. Now he hurried home to the restaurant for his daily meal, carrying with him a small package of books for home reading. It was already way after lunchtime in the restaurant. Only several porters sat at a table with beer mugs in their hands. Nohum's mother moved around wiping the oilcloth covers of the tables with a wet cloth.

"Where have you been all morning?" Itte yelled. "See how pale you are, and dusty all over! You would do better to stay here and help out in the store! Today's children..."

Soon her motherly love took over and made her forget all grudges. Through the low door she quickly entered the back room and returned with a hot dinner plate. Nohum enjoyed the tasty meat patty with the fried potato slices and drank a half a glass of cold beer. He thought of his mother and her devotion to him and the whole family. He felt remorseful; he should have helped in the family business, especially now, in the summer season.

However, next day he forgot his regrets and sneaked out again right after breakfast with a few of his newly acquired books and periodicals into Pinai's villa. There he lay on the soft grass under a shady tree and read again till afternoon.

Chapter 20
THE SLAP

Several weeks after graduation, Nohum was still undecided what to do with himself. Should he forsake his dream about further studies and settle for an apprenticeship in one of the workshops in the neighbourhood? Moshe-Avrohom, too, was beginning to worry about his son's future. Somehow he had heard about Nohum's attendance at meetings of the Workers' Union and he was afraid of the influence these free-thinkers would have upon his son. He suspected that Nohum was already disregarding the obligatory male observances of daily prayer and putting on the phylacteries each weekday morning. He decided to check it out. Next morning, after Nohum came into the restaurant for his breakfast, Moshe-Avrohom asked him quietly:

"Did you recite the morning prayers?"

Nohum put down the buttered roll he was beginning to eat and stammered, "Yes...I recited..."

"And the tefillin, did you put them on?" Moshe-Avrohom inquired further.

"The tefillin..." Nohum flustered, "Yes, I had them on..."

"Go bring them here!" Moshe-Avrohom commanded. Confounded and scared, Nohum did not move from his place, realizing that he was trapped by his lies.

"Go bring the tefillin," Moshe-Avrohom repeated. "The ones that you put on this morning."

Nohum went into the back room and began to search in the drawer where he kept the small velvet bag with the phylacteries. Soon he returned to the store, scared and empty-handed.

"I can not find them...don't know what had happened..." Nohum uttered.

"Liar! Full blown goy!" Moshe-Avrohom roared and smacked Nohum in the face. Nohum wobbled and caught the edge of the nearby table to keep himself from falling down. Sparks fluttered before his eyes and his father's heavy slap burned painfully on his cheek. He was deeply shaken and filled with defiance and rebellion. "Murderer! I am leaving your house!" he shouted and ran from the restaurant.

For some time, Nohum walked the neighbouring streets still feeling the pain and shame of the slap.

"What does he think," Nohum argued resentfully, "he can beat me up as if I were still a Heder boy? I am nearly fifteen years old. I will not let myself be treated like that! I will leave home and be on my own." But where could he go? To whom could he turn for help? He had left home without even one zloty in his pocket, and he was already tired and hungry. After some thinking, Nohum decided to proceed to the railway station where he might help some passenger carry his luggage and earn something for his next meal.

The spacious station was nearly empty. A few porters were walking around slowly, awaiting the arrival of the next passenger train from Warsaw. After a while, the train came in, and they quickly took up position at the exit, ready to offer their services.

Passengers with all kinds of baggage began to file out through the doors into the station. A stocky middle-aged man with a bald pate passed the gate carrying a wooden photography case in one hand, and a folding metal stand with a large picture folder in the other. As he came into the station, he put the case down on the floor, and began to look around as if searching for someone. He noticed Nohum and called him over.

"Will you help me carry around this camera, young man?" he asked Nohum in Polish. "I am a portrait maker from Warsaw. I have come down here for two days to do business. I'll pay you three zlotys a day." He spoke in a friendly manner. "Good! I agree!" Nohum rejoiced at the offer. He lifted the wooden case with his right hand and assured the photographer that it was not heavy at all.

"Heavy it is," the man replied, "but it won't harm you. You are young and have strong muscles. I, too, will have enough to carry." He pointed to the stand and the large folder in his hand. Nohum picked up the wooden case and both left the station. They went along the square where the droshky drivers waited for their passengers, passed under the second railway bridge, and climbed the flight of stairs that led to Warshawska Street where the richer section of the city began.

All day long Nohum walked beside the photographer over the tree-lined avenues and lanes of the upper part of the city. They entered private villas and cottages surrounded by flower beds and grassy paths. Nohum waited at the gate, while the photographer entered and offered his services. Many refused politely, but some let themselves be persuaded and ordered portraits from old photographs or snaps taken on the spot. While the photographer did his work, Nohum rested on the grass or on a bench nearby, observing the opulent surroundings and comparing them with his own poverty-stricken Swiderska Street. One and the same city—he wondered—and how different these places are! Here, people live in clean, spacious cottages with trees and garden beds around them, while there whole families are crowded in one or two rooms, in poverty and in dirt. Would it ever be possible for the inhabitants of Swiderska Street to enjoy life like these people here? he asked himself.

Along the way, Nohum told the photographer about his quarrel with his father and, little by little, of his radical convictions. The man listened attentively without interrupting his outpouring. Then he said: "Poor boy! Why are you worrying for the whole world? Worry for yourself, instead. Go back home, learn a trade and become a man! Life is so short, live and enjoy it! Everything, except the passing moment, is a dream, is vanity." "If life is a dream," Nohum answered, "shouldn't the dream be universal and beautiful? Should it not be about a better morrow for the underprivileged and deprived as well?" The photographer smiled but argued no more.

Towards the evening, they returned to the centre of the city, where the photographer was staying in a guest house. The man paid Nohum his daily salary and told him:

"Come again tomorrow. Afterwards I'll return to Warsaw and you, to your father. Together you'll build up a large workshop. Be here eight in the morning, sharp."

Tired from dragging the heavy case all day, Nohum walked slowly towards his home. Maybe the man was right, he pondered. He should return home and help out his father in the restaurant and in the workshop. In this way, they could build up the family's fortunes. It was already dark when he reached the porter's square where Swiderska Street began. There he met Faivel, the son of the little weird man who lived on the upper floor in Nohum's apartment building. In his childhood, Nohum had played or sometimes fought with Faivel. Over the years, Faivel had grown up into a tall blonde boy, well dressed, and already working as a messenger in a drugstore. Now they both kept a friendly distance, realizing that they cherished different ideals and causes. Nohum told Faivel about his running away from home and his work for the photographer.

"I know about it," Faivel interrupted him wryly, "your mother was all over looking for you."

"I can not go home, Felek," Nohum stated sadly.

"If you can't go home, stay overnight in my shed, in the yard," Faivel said.

"That's what I'll do," Nohum answered. "I'll not return home tonight."

He followed Faivel into the courtyard to a row of wooden sheds huddled along the high fence. Faivel unlocked one of them and let Nohum in.

"Here is your hotel," he said mockingly. "I'll let you out early in the morning before I leave for work."

Nohum remained alone in the dark cell of the shed. In the centre of it was a wooden board on two stands and he lay down on it, putting his shoes under his head for a pillow. He could not fall asleep till deep in the night. From the neighbouring cells he heard frightening noises; cats were jumping somewhere, whining and meowing. What would become of him? Nohum thought. Why had he run away from home and caused so much trouble and sorrow for himself and for his father and mother? But how else could he act? His father had no right to slap him. He could argue, chastise him, but not smack him in the face. He, Nohum, had no choice but to react strongly to remind his father that he was not a child anymore. Anyway, what crime had he committed? Did God need his prayers? Did he need the black phylactery boxes with their leather straps to be worn every morning? Weren't these man-made customs and observances that had outlived their time?

Somehow Nohum fell asleep on the hard plank until early morning, when grey strips of light began to penetrate the cracks of the shed. He rose, took down the plank of the cot, and placed it along the wall and waited for Faivel to release him. Faivel arrived in time, unlocked the door, and looked in at Nohum. "Are you still alive?" he asked with a grin.

"Alive and well, as you can see," Nohum tried to be cheerful.

"Will you come again tonight?"

"Yes, Faivel. One more night, then I'll return home. Wait for me about ten in the evening beside the water pump at the square in front of the house." Nohum left the shed and slunk into the vaulted gate of the building. Here he was accosted by old Horonzik, the janitor, who was wiping the paved entrance to the courtyard with his long broom.

"Hey, young Pan! Your mother is looking for you all over!" called Horonzik in Polish. Without answering him, Nohum went ahead into the street and from there he entered the bazaar. Here he washed his hands and face at the water pump beside the fishmongers stalls and stopped at one of the food stands to buy a fresh buttered roll with Swiss cheese. He then hurried to Koscielna Street to meet the photographer.

Freshly shaved and rested, the photographer was waiting for Nohum in front of the guest house. Nohum grabbed the wooden case and they both proceeded along Warszawska Street towards the town of Srodborow, several kilometers south of Otwock, which had developed during the last decade into a luxurious resort. It lay on the left side of the railway tracks on a picturesque tract of land dotted with young groves, fields, and hills. While Otwock was wrapped in a coat of greenery, Srodborow lay open, pert and saucy, in a sea of sunlight. Here, well-to-do professionals and government clerks built themselves exclusive two-storey homes, surrounded by flower beds and wire fences. Warsaw industrialists and nouveau riche merchants followed suit with miniature flat-roofed palaces. New streets were cut through the fields and groves, and stores were opened to serve the growing population of the new town. Several luxury hotels and guest-houses sprang up providing employment for many Otwock artisans, cooks and waiters, as well as local food suppliers.

All day long Nohum walked with the photographer over the sunny Srodborow streets. They entered newly built spacious houses and hotels surrounded by tended gardens and play-grounds. Men and women in colourful swimsuits were sunbathing on terraces; others were playing cards at tables under coloured umbrellas. Beside the buildings, on tennis courts, young men and women, dressed in white shorts and jerseys, were hitting the tennis balls with zest. Inside the dining halls, waiters hurried with trays full of delicious food.

118

It was the first time in his life that Nohum had seen such luxury, and he could not help but compare what he was seeing with conditions in his poor Swiderska Street. There, in his one room home, six souls were squeezed between his father's sewing machines and mother's kitchen. And yet, his family was still not considered among the poor ones, because they didn't go around hungry and in rags, as many other dwellers of that section did. Why? Why all this inequality? Must it always be this way?

Nohum remembered how Moshe Gelman once said that when the social revolution arrived, he would not pity any bourgeoisie. Their bellies may be opened and thrown to the dogs—and he would still not pity them! Nohum disagreed, saying that the revolution must preserve its moral essence and avoid unnecessary cruelties and bloodshed. Now, seeing with his own eyes the high living style and affluence of the rich, he still did not feel any hatred against these people. They were—he thought—part and parcel of an unjust system into which they were born. The system should be changed and those who defend it must be fought, but no innocent people, rich or poor, should bear the guilt and the suffering...

It was late afternoon when the photographer decided to take a rest and share a snack with his young assistant. At the table in one of the eateries on the main street, he again began to preach to Nohum his life's philosophy:

"Listen my boy! I see that you are quite intelligent and open-minded. Why then are you wasting your youth and future? The revolution may not arrive at all, or will happen without you, but meanwhile you will lose your youth. How will you go on when you grow older? Who will care for you and support you?"

Nohum listened silently. He did not know what to answer. Soon they returned to the railway station in Otwock. The photographer paid Nohum his daily wages and, before he left, reminded him to think over what he had told him.

For some time Nohum lingered at the station until a policeman came and chased out the loiterers from the hall. Nohum then walked around on the lively strip of Warszawska Street until it darkened. Finally, he returned to the square in front of his apartment to meet Faivel.

"See, I'm a gentleman. I came in time," Faivel greeted him.

"Did Mother look for me again?" Nohum inquired.

"Oh, your mother knows everything. Horonzik, the janitor, told her. They also saw you walking around with a photographer. Will you again stay overnight in my shed?" "Yes, only this night. Tomorrow I'll have to go back home," said Nohum.

"Remember, no more than this night. You can not go on sleeping in my shed. Your parents will find out and blame me for everything," Faivel warned him.

Nohum again followed his friend into the dark shed.

"I left an old coat for you to cover yourself with," Faivel said. "What more should I do for you? Provide you with a girl?"

"Thanks, Felek, for everything. I won't forget it," Nohum said as Faivel locked the door of the cell.

Nohum stretched out on the plank cot, covered himself with Faivel's coat, and tried to sleep. Memories from his childhood suddenly arose in his mind. He remembered the beginning of one summer, after the holiday of Pentecost. The Aramaic poem, Akdomos, he learned in Heder was still fresh in his mind. His uncle Mordecai took him for a short vacation to his home in Sadurki, to meet Grandmother Hannah and the other relatives of the village. The room was full of Jews from the neighbouring cottages who came to hear how Nohum, the Heder boy, recited the whole holiday poem by heart. It happened years ago when he attended Yankel Minsker's Heder and was still a God-fearing boy, much happier than now...

Outside a light rain began to tap on the roof of the shed. Nohum felt lonely and forlorn, alone in the dark squalid shed. He recalled the words of the photographer and decided to return home in the morning. He would make up with his father and from now on, try to help his parents in the store and the workshop.

Early in the morning, Nohum left Faivel's shed with no intention of returning there. He was tired and dishevelled and did not know when and how to go home. Again he left for the bazaar, where he could wash his face at the pump and have a snack at one of the bakery stalls.

It was Friday morning and the merchants and vendors were preparing themselves for the busy market day. Farmers arrived on horse-drawn carts and were immediately surrounded by housewives looking for bargains. At one such wagon, Nohum suddenly noticed his mother, bargaining over the price of a chicken she held in her hands. A feeling of great pity and love for his mother overtook him. This was his mother, Nohum thought, who had carried and nursed him, who had watched over him and protected him as the apple of her eye. And how did he reward her for all this? Nohum stood in his place behind his mother's back, unable to move, wiping the tears from his eyes. Just then, Itte turned around and saw her son.

"Nohumel, my child!" she cried and ran over to embrace him.

"Forgive me, Mother! Forgive!" Nohum stammered through tears.

"Come back home, Nohum," Itte pleaded. "How long will you stay away God-knows-where, like a homeless beggar? Father won't touch you any more." She then took Nohum's hand and led him back home. When they came into the restaurant, Moshe-Avrohom turned away behind the counter. Nohum and his mother entered the back room to the amazement of his sisters and little brother.

"Where have you been so long? We all looked for you," his brother asked him. Itte told the children to leave for the yard so Nohum could rest for a while. Nohum took off his shoes and shirt and threw himself on the bed. After a short while, he fell into a deep sleep.

From her corner at the kitchen stove, Itte heard his breathing and prayed in her heart to the Master of the World that He should guard her firstborn from all peril and evil.

Chapter 21
IN THE YOUTH LEAGUE

Silently Nohum sat down at the sewing machine in the corner and began stitching the leather cuts of summer sandals piled on the board beside. At the table stood Moshe-Avrohom cutting the rounded inserts to keep the back of the sandals stiff and sturdy.

"Here is a package of backpieces," Moshe-Avrohom interrupted the silence. "Good, Father," Nohum said, without stopping the sewing.

Since his return home, Nohum had tried to be helpful in the workshop and in the restaurant. He felt shame and regret for running away from home and spending two nights in the dark shed in the courtyard. For his father's sake, he should have put on these phylacteries for a few minutes each morning. It would not have harmed him or damaged the cause of the Revolution. Nohum recalled the days of his childhood when Father used to cuddle him and speak to him tenderly while lying beside him in bed. Now, his father's face is always tense from worrying how to provide for the family. He, Nohum, is the oldest son and must lend a hand.

Towards the evening on that day, both father and son left the workshop; Moshe-Avrohom went to attend the customers who began to fill the restaurant room, and Nohum hurried to prepare himself for the weekly meeting of his cell in the illegal Communist Youth League he had joined soon after leaving school. His friend, Moshe Gelman, had brought him there and at his suggestion, Nohum was soon appointed secretary of the group.

Nohum would gladly not have attended today's meeting. He was tired from all day's work and still disconcerted from his abortive rebellion against his father. What if he got arrested at one of these meetings? What a new blow would it be for his mother and father! Nohum had no time for further misgivings because Moshe Gelman arrived and urged him: "Come, let's go! It's an important meeting. A representative of the Regional Committee will be there." Hurriedly, Nohum washed his hands and face, put on a clean shirt, and left together with Moshe.

On the street, they met Dovid Sadownik, a former classmate, one of the few with whom Nohum was still close.

"Let's take him with us," Nohum suggested. "I have already spoken to him. He is inclined to give it a try."

"Leave him alone! A soft bourgeois offspring. Not for us." Moshe said.

Dovid approached and greeted both friends with handshakes. "Servus, guys! Can I join you?"

"Come along, Dovid," Nohum encouraged him. "We are going you know where...I have already spoken to you..."

"Don't do in your pants for fear," Moshe warned him rudely.

"Who is afraid? Not me!" Dovid boasted.

The three of them proceeded along a quiet sidestreet and entered the city's park. They walked along a narrow path, passing a few lonely couples on benches beside the water basin. Behind the basin was the rectangular pillar with the bronze bust of Marshal Pilsudski. On the wooden bench behind the monument, several members of the cell were waiting.

"Here, here, the secretary has arrived with two bodyguards at his side," said Rozhka, the only girl in the group. She sat squeezed between Avrum Krolik, from the Workers' Union's Youth Section, and Srulik Teitel, the representative of the Regional Committee of the Communist Youth League. Srulik was one of the most admired activists of the illegal youth movement in the area. He was a good orator, a keen polemicist, as well as an excellent organizer, sharp and agile in any situation. Srulik was also known as the proletarian Don Juan. Red haired, with a short forelock over his elongated face, he bewitched many a girl-comrade in the movement. Often he appeared with two girls at side, and his comrades teased him, to mask their envy.

"Srulik, why do you need two?"

"Two is better than one," Srulik retorted.

"What do the girls find in him?" his friends wondered. "Thin like a herring, red like a tomcat, yet all fall for him madly."

Further, at the end of the bench, sat Pinie Cukerkop. He had an open book on his lap and was glancing in it in the semi-darkness.

"Pinie, what are you reading?" Rozhka inquired.

"Probably the tenth volume of Jean Christophe," Shmulik, her brother who was at the other end of the bench, joked. "Pinie doesn't move without Romain Rolland."

Shmulik was a blonde, cheerful boy with the pure innocent face of a cherub. He and his sister, Rozhka, were the only members of the group whose parents were aware of their belonging to the Youth League. Their father, a poor house painter, had been himself a member of the illegal Jewish Socialist Party, "Bund," during the rule of the tzar. He had participated in illegal meetings and strikes and now did not mind that his children followed in his footsteps.

Moshe Gelman sat down on the ground beside Rozhka trying to lean his head backwards on her lap.

"Rozhka belongs to all of us," he said laughingly.

"Move away, black ogre," Rozhka protested. "I belong to nobody."

"Be quiet," Shmulik intervened, "here comes Little Leon. See how he sways on his short feet." All looked up and saw Leon approaching. He came over, greeted everyone with an energetic handshake, and said: "It's not too safe here, comrades. The park attendant must by now know all of us. We'll move to that grove over there."

In pairs, they left the park and entered the grove on the other side of the road. Nohum walked with Dovid who was silent and disheartened all the time.

"Don't be afraid, Dovid. Nothing will happen. You'll get used to it," said Nohum as he led Dovid into the grove. Deeper inside, they found a place to lie down on the grass and began the session. Moshe Gelman, the Chairman of the cell, opened the meeting and called Nohum to deliver the activity report.

"Since the group was founded, less than two months ago," Nohum reported, "weekly meetings are held at which members prepare reviews of current political events and comrade Leon, from the City Committee, gives talks on the theory and practice of Marxism. In addition, two technical meetings were called, devoted entirely to illegal action --distribution of leaflets or slogan writings on walls. As most of the members of the cell are recent graduates from public school, an effort should be made to bring more of their colleagues and friends to the Sabbath afternoon sessions of the Youth Section at the Workers' Union. From there, some of them will find their way into the Youth League --the vanguard of the proletarian youth of Poland."

Srulik, the emissary from the Regional Committee, spoke afterwards, dwelling mainly on the efforts of the Party on behalf of the Spanish Republic, now fighting for its life against the armies of General Franco. A number of comrades from Otwock and Falenica had volunteered to join the International Brigade and had already left for France. From there they will be transported to Spain. One of them, Moniek Swiczarczyk, had fallen on the battlefront, and a memorial meeting in his honour will soon be held at the Workers' Union. All members and sympathizers should be sure to attend. Last but not least, is the ongoing collection for the Spanish cause. Here members of the Youth League should excel and collect whatever donations they can get from comrades, friends, and sympathizers. All members will soon receive the collection lists on which these donations should be noted. The struggle in Spain, Srulik concluded, is a fateful one; it will decide the future of Europe for a long time.

After a brief discussion on both reports, Leon, the political tutor of the group, gave a talk on the theme 'Class Struggle—The Motor of Human History.' The history of the human race, he explained, is the history of class struggle. It's the social motor which moves society forwards. The slaves of antiquity rebelled against their owners; the peasants in medieval times fought their feudal lords. And now the proletarians are battling the bourgeoisie. This struggle turned history into an arena of blood, sweat, and gore. But with the victory of the working class on one-sixth of the globe, the move towards a classless society has already begun.

As Nohum lay on the grass beside Leon, the ardent words of his mentor fired his imagination. He saw in his mind's eye the tremendous clash of the powers of progress and reaction and how the working masses all over the world will, finally, break out of the endless circle of war, destruction, and exploitation. Then all will see that the struggle and effort of the revolutionaries were not for naught. Leon ended his talk and fell silent. Srulik, stretched out on the grass beside, began on a low note a Comsomol love song:

> In Comsomol are girls many,
> But you choose only one at your side.
> You can be a good Comsomoletz
> And love only one in moonlight.

Tell then why, you fell for one
When the moon brightly shone,
Tell, explain it to me
Because it's known all around
That young and budding is our land,
Young and budding every citizen in it.

On the way home, the group split in pairs, each one proceeding by another street. Moshe Gelman left with Dovid, and Nohum walked arm in arm with Leon.

"One has to study, study constantly," Leon said. "The day-to-day work for the Party, in addition to the work for a livelihood, steals all your time. In the long run, if you don't study, you turn into an empty shell."

Soon they reached Leon's apartment inside a villa on Koscielna Street. They climbed the unlit flight of stairs and Leon knocked on the glass door of the anteroom. A petite woman dressed in a light pink housecoat appeared and opened the door.

"This is my Yadzia," Leon introduced his wife, kissing her on the cheek. Yadzia glanced at Nohum and a faint smile appeared on her small, red lips.

"A late-night guest," Nohum said somewhat embarrassed.

"Come in, make yourself at home," Yadzia said, trying to sound friendly.

They all entered the long main room where the couple lived and worked. At the entrance, along the left side wall, was a wooden closet and beside it a straw-twisted bookcase with a radio on top of it. Next came the wide sofa bed that stretched to the window at the end of the room. Along the opposite wall was a small table with three chairs and a sewing machine.

Nohum and Leon sat down on the sofa bed, while Yadzia lit the Primus on the table to prepare a cup of tea for her husband and his guest.

"Nohum is my new pupil, Yadzia," Leon said.

"I am afraid he won't learn any good from you," Yadzia answered, more in earnest than joking. When they sat around the table, Leon began to chat about their life in Warsaw where they had lived before they settled here. They met at the Esperanto Club while Leon was delivering a lecture. That evening, Yadzia fell in love with him and was ready for his sake to leave her well-to-do home and parents.

"You do not regret it, Yadzia," Leon said as he embraced Yadzia.

"It's too late for regrets," Yadzia answered and freed herself from Leon's arms.

It was close to midnight and Leon adjusted his radio to catch the sound of the Internationale with which the Soviet radio stations concluded their nightly programs. Both Leon and Nohum felt pride and joy as they listened to the familiar tune carried over the air.

"History is not standing still," Leon remarked. "It's moving forward— towards Socialism."

Nohum said goodbye to his hosts and left. Down on the empty street, the cool breeze and the scary silence brought him back to reality. In the local police station at the corner, the lights were burning brightly. Two policemen stood outside, at the gate, and looked at Nohum with suspicion. What if they call him back and lock him up in one of those dark cells behind their office? Nohum thought with apprehension. He hastened his steps and continued to walk without looking back. Soon he reached the empty courtyard and slunk on this tiptoes into the back room, where the family lay asleep. He found his folding cot in the dark and lay awake for a long time.

Chapter 22
THE ARREST

Bent over the sewing machine, Leon listened to Nohum, who was sitting beside him, reading aloud from the densely printed pages of the latest issue of 'The New Review,' the illegal monthly of the Communist Party of Poland. It was an article by Yosif Visarionovitch Stalin, Secretary General of the All-Soviet Communist Party, on the Stakhanov movement in the Soviet Union. Work, Stalin claimed, was since time immemorial a curse, instead of the blessing it was meant to be. Through work, the toiling masses were downtrodden and enslaved; it robbed them of all life's joy and turned them into silent, submissive automatons. Not so now, in the Soviet Union, where the working class is engaged in the great building process of a new Socialist society. Here, work is a source of pride and honour, both for the individual worker, as for the collective of which he is a part. No wonder then that thousands of ordinary workers are welcoming the call of the miner Aleksey Stakhanov to raise productivity and tackle higher norms in all branches of industrial and agricultural production. The inspiring call for Socialist competition is now sounded all over the country...

The anteroom doorbell suddenly rang sharply. Nohum interrupted reading and handed over the issue to Leon, who hid it right away in a pile of cut up material on the floor, beside the machine. Leon opened the door and Shmulik Melamed entered.

"I knew that I'll find both of you here," he exclaimed. "The Rebbe with his pupil studying the Torah..."

"Sit down and you'll learn something," said Nohum. "Let's finish the article. It's by Stalin, on the Stakhanov movement."

"Don't bother me with articles," Shmulik replied, "I didn't come for that. Srulik sent me to pick up the Spanish collection-lists and distribute them around the town. I am going first of all to Srodborow to leave some with Rachel, one of our new members. In the Srodborow hotels there are some rich guys, leftists, who support our cause. Will you join me, Nohum?"

Leon went into the anteroom and took from a hidden place in the wall, an envelope with the handwritten lists, and gave it to Shmulik. Tired of sitting and reading to Leon for some time, Nohum decided to join Shmulik in the walk to Srodborow.

"Wait Shmulik. I'm going with you. Together it will be more pleasant. In case they pick us up, one can share in the other's misfortune..."

Still, it was a pity to leave the new issue of the party's journal at Leon's place. From childhood, Nohum felt a magical attachment to the printed word in which one may find truth and understanding. Nohum began nagging Leon to loan him the issue.

"Tomorrow you'll have it back," he assured him. "I'll read it tonight, for sure." Leon hesitated a while, but gave in.

"Be careful, Nohum," he said, "it's hot merchandise..."

Shmulik and Nohum left Leon's apartment and proceeded towards Warszawska Street which lead to Srodborow. At the outskirts of the city, they cut through a pine grove into a lane that would take them to the main street of Srodborow. Engaged in a lively discussion of the military and political situation of the Spanish Republic, the boys did not notice that they were passing the gate of a small villa which housed the police station of Srodborow. Suddenly, they heard a stern voice calling after them: "Stay! Do not move further!" Nohum and Shmulik turned around and saw a tall policeman running towards them.

"Come in, fellows! Let's check who you are and what you are doing here." The policeman led them into the office and immediately began to search both suspects. Quickly he turned out their pockets, opened their shirts, and checked their underwear, shoes and socks. Soon all their possessions lay on his desk, among them the envelope with the handwritten lists and the printed issue of the party journal.

"We are trapped, Nohum," Shmulik murmured.

Nohum did not answer. With head down, he stood overwhelmed by this sudden downfall. "It happened, it happened," he repeated to himself. "Now the main thing is not to break down, not to give out Little Leon..." "Shmulik, remember," Nohum whispered, "No squealing. Not a word..."

"Quiet!" hollered the policeman, "Do not utter a word!"

He then opened the envelope and examined the lists. When he found *The New Review* and skimmed its densely printed pages, his face lit up angrily.

"Aha, Commies, real Commies..." he shouted. Immediately he pulled the black leather ribbon of his police cap under his chin, locked the office, and led the two boys to the Srodborow train station. A half an hour later, they arrived at the Otwock police Commissariat. Several policemen surrounded the two youngsters and began to ridicule and revile them.

"Real Jew-Commies! Damned be their fathers!"

"How old are you, little Bolsheviks? How many red flags did you hang lately?"

"Here you will sing out everything, little birds."

After the Srodborow policeman reported the particulars of the arrest and handed over the evidence to the officer in charge, the two offenders were thrown into separate cells in the back of the police station.

Nohum spent three days on the hard bunk in the pitch black police cell, where only a faint streak of light penetrated through the small barred window near the ceiling. Bundled in his light summer jacket, he lay and pondered how and from where to draw strength to stand up to the supreme test of a revolutionary—not to give out his comrades. Let them torture him, let them cut him to pieces, he repeated to himself, he will not betray Little Leon, from whom he received the illegal issue.

On the way to Otwock, Nohum and Shmulik had managed somehow to work out their version of defence: both the list and the magazine were given to them the other day by an unknown man, whom they never saw again. Thus Nohum claimed and repeated again and again when he was brought for investigation to the head of the police station. The elderly well-mannered Pole appealed to Nohum to save himself and his friend from a trial, and a possible prison term, by disclosing the name of the person who had provided them with the illegal items. But neither his friendliness nor his threats could force either Nohum or Shmulik to change their original statements.

In the evening on the day of their arrest, several plainclothes men came to search Nohum's and Shmulik's homes. They entered Moshe-Avrohom's restaurant and proceeded into the back room, closing the doors to the street and backyard. Moshe-Avrohom stood petrified, hardly believing his own eyes. He had a premonition that a great disaster was going to befall him and his family. He should have foreseen all this from the conduct of his son since he left school, and even before. He was angry at himself for being weak and unable to prevent the boy's downfall. "Such urchins," he fumed, "can not earn even a few zlotys on their own, yet know how to play revolutionaries against the government and the established order and, thus, provoke more anger and hatred against the Jews. He was too soft," Moshe-Avrohom blamed himself. "He had given in too easily and allowed the boy to go his own way. He should not have been afraid when he ran away from home. Let him run wherever he wants. The shame and heartache of this arrest is more than he and his wife can bear..."

As if she was reading his mind, Itte came over to her husband as soon as the search was over and pleaded to have pity on their own child.

"We have to save him...our son...our Kaddish...He will yet find his way. I believe in him. Meanwhie they'll beat and torture him. Do something. I beseech you!"

And Moshe-Avrohom did not rest. The main thing was to see that Heniek, the police agent known as the main Communist baiter, should leave the two youngsters alone. Through a Pole, a long-standing patron of his restaurant, Moshe-Avrohom sent his pleadings, together with a fine food package, to Heniek asking him not to abuse the boys. It worked; nobody at the police station lifted a hand against either of the youngsters. Not being able to squeeze out any new information from the arrested, the Commissar decided to transport them for further investigation to the Regional Police Headquarters in Warsaw.

Both boys were handed over to a policeman to take them by train to Warsaw. At the gate of the police station, Nohum's mother, his two younger sisters and brother were waiting. Sobbing aloud, Itte ran towards Nohum as if to rescue him from his captor. Behind her were her children, all crying and calling Nohum's name. Nohum turned to his mother as if to comfort her, but more than the word "Mame" he could not utter. The policeman took both boys by their arms and led them hurriedly across the street, through the side entrance to the railway platform.

Nohum sat in the corner of the coach shrunken and subdued. With eyes closed, he saw again and again his mother's distressed face and heard her helpless sobbing. Was it right, even in the name of the loftiest ideal, to cause so much aggravation and pain to those who loved him and cared for him so much? Had he the right to ignore his family's suffering, even if he did not care for his own well-being? These questions tormented him even later on, when he was thrust into a cell at the Regional Police Headquarters in Warsaw.

On the hard bunk, all alone in the small cell, Nohum lay dozing and mulling over his predicament. From time to time he was taken out and led through long corridors into the investigator's office. Here again he was steadfast, prepared at all costs not to betray Leon or his other comrades. Nohum realized that the investigators will not use torture on them because he and Shmulik were minors, boys in their fifteenth year. He soon got used to the threats and verbal abuse and it did not bother him any more. He was expecting to be tried and sentenced to a prison term of a year or two. It was a hard price, but he was prepared to pay it rather than involve any of his comrades.

Tired and exhausted from the investigation, Nohum was brought back to his cell and he lay again on the bunk, looking for hours at the small, grated window on the wall beneath the ceiling from where a piece of the sky could be seen. There, outside the prison walls, life was flowing freely, with its joys and sorrows—and all this he suddenly lost some ten days ago. "O freedom,"—he paraphrased the famous lines of Adam Mickiewicz—"you are like health that can be appreciated only by one who loses you."

Twice a day the door opened and the guard brought a bowl of thick soup with a chunk of black bread, which Nohum swallowed eagerly. He then returned to his bunk to endure the monotonous, dragging hours of waiting to see what would happen next. On the tenth day of his arrest, Nohum was taken out and led under guard to the prison yard. Here he saw for the first time since they were brought to Warsaw, his friend Shmulik Melamed. Shmulik smiled faintly and nodded twice to Nohum as he passed by under a policeman's guard, thus letting him know that everything was well: he had not told on anybody.

The two policemen led the boys outside the Regional Compound, several blocks away, to the Headquarters for political prisoners on Danilewiczowska Street. The large waiting room there was full of arrested men and the policemen guarding them.

Silent and strained, the haggard prisoners sat on benches or squatted on the floor, waiting for the ritual of being photographed and fingerprinted. Nearly all of them were smoking heavily and the air was filled with the stench of sweat and smoke.

It took more than an hour until Nohum's term arrived. He entered a room where two clerks quickly took his fingerprints and led him to the photography room where he was told to climb a high chair with an attached number in front of it. Here he was photographed several times from the front, left and right profiles, and from the front again. Finally, he was told to return to his guard in the waiting room. The policeman brought him back to the Regional Detention Center, to his cell.

Several more days passed without anything happening. Then, one afternoon, Nohum was taken out of his lock-up and led to the main office. There he saw his father standing, cap in hand, beside the desk of a civilian dressed clerk.

"Here is your son," the official said. "Please sign the warranty that he won't get involved in any more illegal activities." Moshe-Avrohom bent down and signed the paper.

"You are now free to take him home," the man said. "But remember, it's your responsibility to watch and guide him. To have children is no great deal, a cat does it, too. But to bring them up the proper way—that's the thing!"

The official handed over the release paper to Moshe-Avrohom and walked them to the door of his office. Moshe-Avrohom shook his hand and thanked him. Hurriedly and with great relief, father and son left the compound to return to home and freedom.

Chapter 23
DISILLUSIONMENT

On the way home from jail, Nohum gave his father a solemn promise that, as long as he was staying with his family, he would not renew his activities in the illegal youth organization.

Soon after, Moshe-Avrohom found an apprenticeship for Nohum with one of the better boot-stitchers in the area. From then on, Nohum spent his weekdays in the workshop of Sinai Goodman, on Merchant Street, across from the House of Study. The shop was located in the small kitchen of the two-room dwelling which Sinai shared with his wife and little daughter. The left corner, beside the entrance, was the domain of Hancia, Sinai's wife; there she cooked and baked for her family. The rest of the room, along the window to the street, was taken up by the two sewing machines and Sinai's cutting table.

At the sewing machine to the right sat the operator Shimele, a man in his early thirties, with a scrawny, pock-marked face and small, hidden eyes. In his younger years, he was active in the Workers' Union, especially in its drama-circle. There he learned a variety of Yiddish songs, which he loved to sing and hum while sewing the leather uppers. But all this belonged to the past, before Shimele became engaged to a maiden from a respectable, religious home and, for her sake, he had to start behaving himself properly. Since then, he stayed away from his comrades in the Union and, from time to time, even attended synagogue on Sabbath mornings with his future father-in-law.

Sinai Goodman was a smiling, good-natured fellow who enjoyed life in general, and his wife and little daughter in particular. Without embarrassment, and in front of all, he would hug and pat his stout Hancia.

Sinai was known as a good boot-stitcher and Moshe-Avrohom had hoped that at his place, Nohum would learn a better workmanship than in his own rundown workshop. Although Nohum had known the rudiments of the trade from watching or sometimes helping his father, Sinai did not trust him to do the stitching of the fine leatherware with which he dealt. Thus Nohum spent all winter at Sinai's place, doing minor jobs and not really mastering the trade. Still, Sinai found the boy useful and soon began to pay him a minimal apprenticeship wage of ten zlotys per week.

When free from work, Nohum indulged in serious reading, in Yiddish and in Polish. He was a regular visitor at Wasserzug's lending library on Warszawska Street. Wasserzug, an old radical and secularist, guided Nohum in choosing from the best in world literature, in Yiddish and Polish translations. From time to time, Nohum attended the Sabbath afternoon meetings of the Youth Section or the Friday night discussion forums at the Workers' Union. However, in spite of urgings from comrades, Nohum kept his vow not to return to the illegal youth organization.

Whenever he could, Nohum visited Little Leon's place and often spent long evening hours there, indulging in serious readings and discussions. Leon needed Nohum now more than ever, because, unexpectedly, Yadzia, his wife, had left him and gone back to Warsaw. Rumours had it that she had found herself another lover, also a tailor, but a more settled man than Leon. If this was not enough, Leon suddenly became estranged from the Party and was at odds with his old comrades.

It all began with the arrest of Ben-Zion Kezman, one of the members of the Hasidic cell of the Communist Youth League. This circle consisted of youngsters from the most religious and respectable families in town. Its members and sympathizers included the city's Hasidic Rabbi's younger sister, one of the sons of the government appointed Rabbi, several sons and daughters of ritual slaughterers, well-to-do merchants and butchers. All of them led a double life, conducting themselves fittingly in their homes, while at the same time, they were deeply involved in revolutionary thought and action. Dressed in their traditional gaberdines and Jewish caps, they used to meet once or twice a week in a private apartment of one of their own, discussing Marxist theory, socializing and flirting. One of these young men was Ben-Zion Kezman, a gentle-looking, quiet youngster, barely nineteen years old, still wearing the traditional garb and short earlocks hidden behind his ears.

Ben-Zion was the son of a butcher shop owner in the bazaar. Because he chose to be a Torah student and not a butcher like his brothers, he was pampered by his parents and provided with everything he needed. Thus Ben-Zion had ample time and means to serve the revolutionary movement and to perform for its sake the most dangerous missions. One of these was to provide illegal literature to Demblin, a city halfway to Lublin. In the Demblin fortress, a large Polish army garrison was stationed and it was of utmost importance to provide the underground army cells with communist literature. This task was assigned to Ben-Zion and he proudly fulfilled it.

Dressed in his Hasidic outfit, he travelled by train to Demblin, carrying a large suitcase with illegal propaganda material. There he delivered it to a Polish railway worker, a trusted party member, who knew where and for whom the material was destined. These trips continued for some time without a hitch, until the conspiracy was broken up and Ben-Zion was arrested.

This happened in the spring of 1937, a week before Passover. Ben-Zion arrived, as usual, at the railway man's place and was told by the wife to sit and wait while she called her husband. She soon returned with a military gendarme at her side and Ben-Zion was arrested. Later on, the Otwock Party found out that the railway worker was having an affair for some time with another woman and his wife, enraged by her husband's unfaithfulness, betrayed both him and her young Jewish comrade. Meanwhile, Ben-Zion was transported to the Political Section of the Lublin police, known for its harsh treatment of subversives. There he endured merciless beatings and tortures, but did not give anyone away. Finally he was put behind bars in the Lublin jail to await his trial.

And here, Leon's troubles with the city's Party Committee began. Ben-Zion's mother somehow learned about Leon, that he was her son's mentor, and she began to visit him, demanding that the Party provide her son with a reliable attorney. She was an energetic and quite intelligent woman and her demands were restrained and reasonable. However, when Leon brought her case before the Party Committee, he was sharply criticized by his comrades. He had no right, Leon was told, to admit to that woman that he was in any way connected to or responsible for her son's arrest. Furthermore, he should not have promised her to obtain funds for a lawyer, because the established policy was to help only members from poor, proletarian families, and not sons of the well-to-do. In the heat of the argument, Leon exclaimed:

"Comrades. I see that with you a man is no more than a lemon; you squeeze out his juices and throw away the shell!"

"These are words of a renegade of the working class, and not of a conscious Communist," the Chairman of the meeting declared.

"Such is my life's work and such its reward," Leon retorted bitterly.

A dead silence fell in the room. The Chairman called the meeting to an end, and one by one, the comrades left without uttering a word to Leon.

However, Ben-Zion's mother continued to visit Leon, insisting that he should provide help for her son. Leon did not know what to answer and tried to avoid her. Several times, in Nohum's presence, he hid himself beforehand in the wooden closet, but the woman kept on waiting so long, until Leon had to come out embarrassed and shamefaced.

Leon tried once more to appear before the Committee of the Party, but to no avail; all contacts with him were cut off. Little Leon, the fervent and dauntless Communist was now branded an 'enemy of the people,' a follower of the right-wing Zinoviev-Bukharin gang, who were at that time tried and sentenced to death in Moscow.

At Leon's apartment, Nohum and Leon pored with disbelief over the densely printed pages of Chief Procurator Wyshinski's ravings against the Trotskyite, Zinoviev-Bukharinite gang of murderers, wreckers and spies. At first, Leon wavered and even tried to defend the Party line. Did not Stalin foretell, in January 1933, that the desperate resistance of the defeated classes would increase, as the Soviet state approaches the final stages of Socialism? Nohum was confused and doubtful. Together they continued to analyze and weigh the pros and cons of the whole matter, and soon began to express their doubts aloud. Wasn't Leon too, here in Poland, branded an 'enemy of the people' by his own comrades? All the confessions must have been forced out from the accused by torture, threats to their families or other means, both of them concluded. The Moscow trials seemed to be no more than a personal vendetta against Stalin's former critics, or a brutal attempt to usurp all power, as Bonaparte did after the French Revolution.

Still, Leon found consolation in the humanist foundations of Communism. Unlike Fascism, which preaches unabashedly hatred to and submission of other nations, the essence of Communism is the renewal and the solidarity of the human race. Like Christianity, Communism must return to its pristine foundations or perish.

"A time will come," Leon foretold, "when Stalin and his henchmen will be no more, and all these innocent people, arrested, tortured, and executed, would be exonerated and rehabilitated. History," Leon concluded, "does not like foul deeds. Eventually, truth would rise like oil on water's surface."

"But meanwhile," Nohum excitedly exclaimed, "meanwhile millions will have died, and no one will be able to restore their lives or reverse the anguish and pain of their families. We have served a false god, Leon, a Molokh who devours his own offspring..."

Leon nodded and silently agreed with his pupil.

Soon after the second Moscow trial, a meeting was called by the leaders of the Workers' Union to denounce the renegades and slanderers of the Soviet Union outside and inside the workers' ranks. The two rooms of the Unions' premises were fully packed and some even stood outside, at the open windows and doors. At the head table were members of the city's Party Committee and the Youth League, as well as other union activists. One by one, speakers denounced the bourgeois and Social Democratic heretics who were having a field day in slandering the Soviet Union. A resolution calling for the elimination from the workers' ranks of traitors, Trotskyites and Social-Fascists of all kind was read and accepted by applause.

Nohum was present at the meeting but did not dare to come out openly against the speakers or the resolution. However, when Asher Silver came forth with a proposal to expel Little Leon from the Unions' Cultural Committee and Youth Section, Nohum rose from his place and walked out of the room. He was already at the start of Swiderska Street when he heard somebody from behind calling his name. Nohum turned around and saw Moshe Gelman running towards him.

"Wait, Nohum," Moshe called. "I'm with you! No more a member of the Youth League!"

Chapter 24
BUNDISTS

All through the summer, the circle around Leon continued to grow. Moshe Gelman followed Nohum, and soon Pinie Cukerkop joined them. As if from nowhere appeared Avrum Kleinman, a tall boy with an elongated gentle face and a wide forehead. He was the son of a well-to-do watchmaker who could afford to send his boy to the gymnasium, a privately owned High School, which only a few Jewish youngsters attended. Avrum possessed a broad, intellectual outlook and a logical way of thinking through a problem, and he was respected for these qualities by his comrades.

On Sabbath afternoons, sometimes even on weekday summer evenings, the group would find a quiet nook in the park, or a bench on Kosciuszko Avenue, and delve into lengthy discussions on the nature of Communism and Democratic Socialism. All of them agreed that in the Soviet Union, under Stalin, the Dictatorship of the Proletariat had turned into a dictatorship over all the working classes, and that the Party itself had become an oppressive tool of the dictator and his clique.

On several occasions, the group heard talk of anarcho-syndicalism from a couple, Leon's friends from Warsaw, who used to visit him from time to time. Pinie and his wife, Eva, were well known in the Anarchists' circles in Warsaw as idealists who devoted their time and energy to the dissemination of anarchist thought. Pinie was of medium height, sturdy, with a ruddy face, while Eva was taller, with pitch-black hair braided on the back of her head. Pinie was a house-painter by profession, often more unemployed than working. He and Eva lived poorly and paid little attention to their material well-being or manner of attire.

However, their anarchist ideas seemed too vague and unreal to Leon and his disciples. No central government, no judicial or legislative branches, only freely associated and loosely bound social units, all of them living in peace and harmony—all this sounded too good to be true. What remained then were the Polish

Socialist Party or the Bund—its Jewish counterpart. Both of these parties seemed to be lacking, in the eyes of the youngsters, in revolutionary fervour and decisiveness in their struggle for a socialist Poland. But in order to grow and develop into an influential youth organization in town, the group would have to join one of these parties.

A branch of the Polish Socialist Party existed in the city, but it did not have any youth organization. Anyway, there was no point for Yiddish-speaking youngsters to join a Polish party. Only a few assimilated Jews belonged there, participating in activities without acknowledging their Jewishness in particular, or Jewish problems in general. Their only remaining option was to join the youth movement of the Bund, the so-called Youth-Bund "Zukunft" and establish such an organization in Otwock.

The Jewish youth of Otwock and the nearby town of Karczew had been under the spell of either the Zionists or the Communists since the end of the First World War. There were only a few elderly Bundists in town. Years ago, they had formed a "Culture-League" where Yiddish lectures and courses were held; but they lacked leadership and devoted members, and soon disappeared into oblivion.

However, in Warsaw, as in many larger and smaller cities, the Bund had managed to build a broad and powerful workers' movement since Poland won its independence. Founded in 1897, the year of the first Zionist congress, the "General Workers' Bund of Poland and Lithuania" was an autonomous party within the wider framework of the Russian Social Democratic Party. Under the tzars, the Bund was involved in workers' strikes and other illegal activities, and played an important role in the revolution of 1905. At that time, the Bund had its charismatic leaders as well as its martyrs, widely known all over the Russian empire.

The October Revolution put an end to the Bund as to the other Social Demo-cratic or bourgeois parties in Russia. The party was split from within by those who wanted to join the Bolshevik band-wagon; others were arrested or exiled by the Communist security forces; and many fled to Poland. Here the Bund had rebuilt itself and established a youth and children's movement, workers' un-ions, a net of secular Yiddish schools, sports clubs, and cultural as-sociations. In Poland, the Bund had freed itself of its neutrality in matters of assimilation and fostered Yiddish culture and literature through book-publishing, a periodical press, as well as a daily Yiddish newspaper—*Di Folkstzaytung*—widely read by Jewish workers and the liberal-minded intelligentsia. With the growth of anti-Semitism in Poland in the thirties, and the inability of the Zionists to foster a large-scale emigration to Palestine, the Bund grew in stature as the defender of the Jewish masses and their right to live and work in Poland. Like the Polish Socialist Party, the Bund was a member of the Socialist International and had the status of a legal party, although closely watched and often harassed by the Polish authorities.

While Leon and his comrades were groping with the question of joining the Bund, a newcomer suddenly appeared from Warsaw. His name was comrade Froim, a man who, from his youth on, devoted himself entirely to the working man's cause. He was active in the Communist Youth movement in his hometown, Parczew, where he was arrested and sentenced to several years in prison. After his release, he moved to Warsaw where the fractional infighting between the followers of the party line and the Trotskyite Opposition was at its height. Dismayed with Stalin's brutal suppression of the Opposition, Froim joined the Trotskyite faction in Warsaw, and after a while, he as well as many of his comrades, were admitted to the Bund and became loyal Bundists.

During the years in confinement, comrade Froim had developed tuberculosis and, therefore, decided to move to Otwock, famous for its favourable climate and sanatoria. Here he soon found employment in a barber's shop and began to look around and sound out the possibility of establishing a Bundist organization in town. Thus comrade Froim found his way to Leon and his youth circle. Together they began to plan the opening of the new Youth-Bund in Otwock.

Soon a meeting was arranged in the house of a Bundist couple. There the few elderly Bundists met both Leon and Froim and the young activists with Nohum, Moshe Gelman and Avrum Kleinman at the head. The Bundists could not believe their eyes seeing so many enthusiastic youngsters suddenly appearing as if from nowhere. They eagerly pledged to contribute to a special fund to rent premises where the youth, as well as the older party members, would meet and conduct their activities. By the end of the summer 1938, all formalities with the Central Committee of the Youth-Bund in Warsaw were concluded. Soon a house was found on a side lane near the railway tracks for the new organization.

The rented two rooms with its front porch were newly painted and decorated with Yiddish slogans and portraits of Bundist leaders. Books had been collected and arranged in a case to form the nucleus of a Yiddish library. A friend of Froim, a former music teacher, now a patient in the "Marpeh" Sanatorium, volunteered to lead a youth choir. Youngsters and even smaller children began to flock to the new place and filled the rooms with sound and song till late in the evening.

The official opening of the Bund house was celebrated with a noisy wine and cake party till late in the night. The place was full of young people as well as elderly Bundists and sympathizers. Toasts and short speeches were given by Leon and Froim, followed by songs and declamations by members of the Youth-Bund. The honour of delivering the main talk on the festive occasion was given to comrade Yekusiel. Yekusiel was a man in his middle thirties, tall and portly, with a mild face and slow manner of speech. The thick, dark thatch that adorned his head was streaked with grey lines and added a venerable touch to his figure and demeanor. A qualified boot-stitcher by trade, he delved passionately in his free hours into the treasures of Yiddish literature in all its genres and manifestations. To hear Yekusiel speak on the poetry of Itzik Manger, on the dramas of Leivick, or the novels of Joseph Opatoshu, was a rewarding experience to which Nohum and his comrades looked forward. Yekusiel was a Bundist from his youth and it was natural that to him belonged the honour of being the guest speaker at the opening of the new Bundist house.

Slowly, and in a distinctive manner, comrade Yekusiel elaborated on the essence of Bundist ideology. "Bundism", he said, "is nourished by the creative springs of Jewish life and culture. Because of that, we cherish so much the Yiddish language and its modern literature. Both of them—the spoken tongue and its literature—are the inheritors and continuators of Jewish creativity since the Bible. Our longing and striving for a Socialist society has its roots not only in the modern socialist theories, but no less in the preaching and visions of the great Hebrew prophets. Our decisive effort for the existence and continuation of the Jewish people is rooted in the thoughts and deeds of our saints and martyrs of all ages.

"We love and accept our people as they are and wherever they are. Thus, unlike the Zionists, we do not specify conditions for the normalcy of our people. We reject the Zionists' 'rejection of the golus' which categorizes the Jewish Diaspora as a lower, unworthy state of existence. We are a world-nation and will remain as such even if a Jewish state in Palestine will come into being. Wherever our people live and dwell, we are with them, promoting positive action, cultural enlivenment, and strengthening of their economic and political positions.

"And as to our program of national and cultural autonomy for each ethnic minority, small or large, it is both a bulwark against assimilation and a rescue program for a world torn by nationalistic rivalries and hatreds.

"So, my dear young friends and older comrades, your work and effort was crowned with success. With the opening of this new Bundist house in Otwock, we kindled a light, a torch of hope and trust in the future of our people and in the victory of a Socialist Society in our country and elsewhere.

"So be proud, comrade Bundists! Rejoice in your achievement and carry on with your noble Bundist work in our city."

After the opening celebration, the new youth-organization continued to grow and soon formed at its side a SKIF—a Socialist Children's Association. At its helm was Nohum, the secretary of the Otwock Youth-Bund. After a long day in the workshop, he would hurry to the Bundist local to conduct talks or attend committee meetings or children's group. The Youth-Bund thus became his second home, his life's endeavour.

With the arrival of spring, the Youth-Bund organization began arranging summer outings. One of the most favoured places to visit was the Medem Sanatorium in Miedzeszyn, a resort place on the Otwock-Warsaw railway line. This exemplary educational institution was the pride of the Bundist movement in Poland and it attracted visitors from all over the country and from abroad.

On a Saturday morning, the Otwock Youth-Bund group would begin the ten kilometre walk on the sandy tract along the railway line to Warsaw. By noon they would usually reach Falenica, a town only a few kilometres from Miedzeszyn. Here they could rest for a while at the local Youth-Bund branch and then proceed to the Sanatorium.

When the group reached the platform of the Miedzeszyn railway station, they could already see from afar the red roof of the sanatorium. Coming closer, the visitors would notice the well-kept lawns and flower-beds that surrounded the health resort. In front of the house was a large enclosed veranda where many children rested on folding beds after lunch. From the veranda, doors led to the spacious dining hall where tables were already being set for the evening meal.

In some of the side rooms, different committee meetings were going on. There, children with some adults from the staff were working on all facets of life in the institution, such as: cleanliness and hygiene, the library, radio programming, and others. They also took care of the chicken incubator, the dovecote, anthill and vegetable garden. Others participated in the choir and drama group which prepared occasional performances and operettas written and composed by the children together with their teachers.

Most of the inhabitants of the sanatorium were children from poverty-stricken Jewish quarters in Warsaw and other cities. Many of them arrived from their congested homes pale-faced and weak, but returned, after a four to six week stay, in better health, rested and enriched with happy and joyful memories.

In special cases, some children remained in the sanatorium for a longer period. Such, at that time, was the case of Shmulik Minkowski, whose parents were murdered during the pogrom in Przytyk. During the attack on their home, Shmulik was hidden in a closet and thus, orphaned from both father and mother, he survived. He was then sent for convalescence to the Medem Sanatorium, before being permanently placed in a Jewish orphanage. At the Medem Sanatorium he was showered with much attention and care from all. Yet he remained withdrawn, still overwhelmed by the tragedy that had befallen him.

As soon as the rest hour was over, the premises of the sanatorium were full of children busying themselves with all of the activities. Some of them attached themselves to the visiting group, guiding them around the place.

Nohum loved to participate in and lead these visits to such a highly sophisticated educational institution. He returned from there revived and strengthened in his belief that a freedom-loving socialist society is not only a historical necessity, but a way of life which could become a reality as well.

Several weeks before Passover, Shaindel suddenly returned from Hachsharah. After nearly seven years of work in different sites of Poland, she was still unable to obtain a certificate of entry into Palestine. However, the Hechalutz Headquarters in Warsaw agreed that she deserved to be sent there illegally, provided she can obtain the sum of seven hundred zlotys to partly cover the expenses of the trip. Shaindel entered the crowded back room behind the restaurant, where she hardly could find a place to put down her two large suitcases. She exclaimed bitterly:

"My God! How can you go on living in such a clutter? We must find a place away from the restaurant!"

Soon after she unpacked her belongings, Shaindel began to rearrange and clean every nook of the back room and the front store as well. Her arrival infused new life into the sluggishness and apathy of the family. For Moshe-Avrohom, raising the sum of seven hundred zlotys to pay for his daughter's journey was a formidable task. This sum had to be saved during the few summer months before the business will come to a standstill. He realized that Shaindel was right: they had to find other living quarters and thus enlarge the restaurant with the back room. He began to look around and soon rented a room across the street, a few steps away from the restaurant.

Again Moshe-Avrohom and Nohum carried the house belongings as well as the sewing machines to the new place. The room was quite large and there was enough place for the beds and closet at the back wall, and the boot-stitching shop beside the window, facing the street.

Meanwhile, Shaindel was busy cleaning and fixing up the enlarged restaurant. From early morning till late at night she was at her post, attending the customers or helping out Itte in the kitchen. She was also helpful in caring for the children, preparing their meals before and after school, or helping them wash and change for the Sabbath.

The summer season seemed to go well. Under Shaindel's management, the restaurant attracted more customers than ever. Former friends from the Hechalutz movement came often to see her and spent time in the store, eating and drinking. From time to time they arranged noisy parties at which they remembered their younger years and friendships.

All day long Nohum continued to work at Sinai's boot-stitching shop and in the evenings he was busy at the Youth-Bund organization. Shaindel, who loved Nohum now as ever, was deeply pained by his belonging to an anti-Zionist youth organization. She wondered how Nohum found his way to the Bundist camp and tried many times to challenge his new beliefs. "Don't you see, Nohum, the hopelessness of our predicament in Poland?" she argued in despair. "We are sitting on a volcano which could erupt any day and bury us in its deadly ashes."

"And what about Palestine, isn't there a volcano also? How would you, Zionists, quell the ongoing Arab rebellion and resistance? Isn't it a struggle of a people which is being dispossessed and turned into a minority in the land of their birth? Are we not giving up the aura of a spiritual nation to become narrow-minded oppressors of another people? Thus we are for sure losing our spiritual birthright without attaining real security!" Nohum argued heatedly.

During these discussions, Nohum and Shaindel often became emotionally embroiled and soon realized that there was no point to continue these sparrings. Both of them were firmly rooted in their respective outlooks and had to continue their separate ways. Only the future would prove whose path was the right one and led to the betterment and alleviation of the suffering of the Jewish people.

The summer passed quickly and at its end, Moshe-Avrohom was able to provide Shaindel with the necessary funds for her journey. It included a tourist excursion to Italy, from where its participants were supposed to embark on an illegal ship that would bring them to the shores of Palestine. The whole affair was to be conducted in secrecy, and Shaindel's departure could not, therefore, be publicized. Only the close family and a few of her girlfriends were at the station when she left. Moshe-Avrohom embraced his daughter beside the train coach and said tearfully: "May God bring you safely to the Land of Israel!"

"I'll come there, Father dear," Shaindel said. "And all of you will join me later on, with the help of the One Above...You'll see..." Trembling with emotion, Shaindel embraced Itte, then Nohum, and the rest of the children. At the whistling of the conductor, Shaindel tore herself away from her dear ones and entered the coach. The train began moving and soon disappeared over the bridge into the faraway world.

A few weeks passed and there was no news from Shaindel. Then a letter arrived from a Kibbutz in Upper Galilee. In it Shaindel described how, under the cover of night, the illegal immigrants were taken off the ship into smaller boats and brought to a lonely spot on the shores of the Mediterranean. From there they were speedily dispersed to different agricultural settlements all over the country. Shaindel, among others, was absorbed into a large and beautiful Kibbutz—the "Morning Star of Galilee". Here she found a new home and a future.

Shaindel's letter was read and re-read many times for the family, friends, and neighbours. All were excited and happy with her success. A new hope was kindled in Moshe-Avrohom's heart: his daughter is now among the builders of the Jewish land. In time, he and his family will leave, too, Poland and begin life anew in the land of their ancestors, in Eretz Israel.

Chapter 25
YOUNG LOVE

Of all the girls in Nohum's class, only Franka had joined the newly founded youth organization. Although from a middle class family—her parents owned a two storey house at the far end of Nohum's street—Franka, too, had felt an inner attachment and solidarity with the poor inhabitants of the Jewish quarter around the bazaar. Like Nohum, she was reprimanded on several occasions by Pani Szymanska, or her husband, for expressing radical ideas in her written assignments.

After graduation, some of her girlfriends found their way to one or another Zionist youth group, while others had begun to visit dancing halls where they could meet young men of their kind. But Franka stayed away from these places. During the day, she helped out in the family business of selling crates of yeast to stores and bakeries in the city. In her free time, she gave a few private lessons, read Polish novels, or met with friends in town or in Warsaw.

For more than two years since the graduation, Nohum had no contact with Franka. When they occasionally met on the street, they greeted each other politely and continued their separate ways. It seemed to Nohum that since he kept her company at the graduation party, Franka avoided him, and he did not have the courage to approach her and find out the reason for it. Meanwhile, he got absorbed with the underground Youth League, then came his arrest, the disillusionment, and his involvement in the formation of the Bundist youth organization. All these made him forget Franka and the few pleasant hours they spent at the graduation evening.

Now, unexpectedly, Franka joined the Youth-Bund and soon became active there, especially with the younger children. It came about mainly because of comrade Froim, who had lived for some time in a small, bachelor apartment on the upper floor of Franka's house. Quiet and gentle, Froim emanated trustfulness and friendship to all those with whom he cared to associate. Thus he persuaded Franka to join the new organization, and here Nohum began to meet her anew. Soon they began to be drawn one to another. It happened on one of those winter nights, when the snow came down gently and covered all the outside in a pure, white attire. After a noisy evening at the Youth-Bund, Nohum walked Franka home. It was near midnight when they entered the dark staircase of Franka's house. All around was quiet and peaceful. The inhabitants of the main and upper floors seemed to be all asleep. Franka's hair was adorned with silvery snowflakes and her eyes shone in the dark. As if by themselves, their hands met and drew their bodies in a close embrace; and their mouths, too, joined in a warm and prolonged kiss. Suddenly Franka freed herself from Nohum's arms, and saying hurriedly 'goodbye' she entered her home.

Nohum walked slowly over the snow-covered street, drunk with a great joy and sudden happiness. "Franka loves me, and I am in love with her," he repeated to himself. This is his beloved, the one and only, that will share his life from now on, he was convinced.

Many evenings followed with Nohum and Franka engaged in long nightly walks over the quiet streets and alleys of the city. The winter months passed quickly and spring arrived with its rich foliage and fragrance of acacia and lilac. The hearts of the young lovers were full of longing and desire.

Now they could engage in long nightly walks over the open sandy stretches on the way to the Swider River. There they would rest on the grass beside a leafy tree and continue their deliberations on life and society, or on books they read. These hearty talks were, naturally, interspersed with hugging, petting and kissing.

Franka's body was full and ripe, her hair soft and her lips fresh and juicy. Her large eyes shone with wonderment and love. Nohum would let his hands wander over her body, gently touching her hair, waist and breasts. But he did not dare to proceed further. When he sometimes did get carried away, he would be stopped by Franka's gentle pleas not to do harm to her.

Nohum was now convinced that his involvement with Franka was the first real love he experienced. His attachment to Dora during the last year in school, he now saw as an expression of his longing for that love. In grade six, before his infatuation with Dora, he had fallen under the spell of another classmate, Sarah, a girl with long, thick braids and a dimpled face. They met only a few times in the evening, after extracurricular school activities. Sarah lived in one of those lanes at the outskirts of the city where the wooden houses were surrounded by small garden plots and trees. There, under an old chestnut tree, Nohum engaged, for the first time, in kissing and petting a girl.

Nohum confessed to Franka his former involvement with Sarah and his naive love for Dora. Also Franka had some experiences of her own to tell. Before she began to go out with Nohum, she was for several months the girlfriend of Nohum's associate, Avrum Kleinman. However, she had found Avrum too aggressive and demanding. They stopped rendezvousing and he soon found a girl of his liking from the left-Zionist "Hashomer" organization. Still, it was hurting him that Franka got involved with Nohum and he used every occasion to criticize Nohum and deride him.

With the coming of summer, Nohum and Franka ventured on Saturday mornings farther beyond the city. On the way, they would stop at farmhouses and buy dark bread and milk. Then they would settle under a tree on a hill overlooking the area and Nohum would bring forth his thick writing book with his poems and prose compositions.

Already in school, in grade six and seven, Nohum had begun to write poems and stories in Polish. He even tried to write a novel about the adventures of two runaway boys, but did not manage to proceed beyond the first few chapters. Under the influence of Pan Perlmuter, the Yiddish-loving religion teacher, Nohum soon began to write in his mother tongue, Yiddish. He also began to familiarize himself with the contemporary Yiddish literature in Poland and abroad through books and various literary journals.

Early in 1939, the Yiddish Scientific Institute of Vilna announced an autobiography contest for young Jewish men and women in Poland. On the basis of these autobiographies, the Institute would gather authentic material on the life and problems of the Jewish youth in the country. Some of the autobiographies were to be awarded and even published.

The idea of participating in this contest excited Nohum greatly. Here was a unique chance to tell all about his life—his childhood years in Heder and in school. In such an autobiography, he would tell not only about himself, but of his family and the people around them. He would also describe the trials and tribulations of his formative years—his involvement in the Communist Youth League, the arrest and the disillusionment in the illegal movement, as well as his contribution to the founding of the Youth-Bund in Otwock. And lastly—of his love affair with Franka. The record of all these phases of his young life were valuable material, not only for the researchers of the Yiddish Scientific Institute, but for himself as well. They may well serve him as a basis for a future work of fiction on the life of the Jewish youth in Poland.

But how could he undertake such an assignment when all his weekdays were spent in the workshop and his evenings—in the local of Youth-Bund and in late night walks with Franka? Only the early morning hours before the beginning of his workday could be utilized for writing. But this could not be done at home, in their one room dwelling, with his siblings awakening early morning, and his father at the sewing machine at dawn. Nohum discussed this matter with Franka and she offered a solution—to rent the vacant one room apartment in her mother's house which has been till lately occupied by comrade Froim. Nohum wholeheartedly agreed and left it to Franka to convince her mother to rent him the room. Goodhearted and tolerant by nature, Franka's mother easily gave in to her daughter's pleadings and the room was given to Nohum for a minimal monthly rent.

Roise, Franka's mother, was a plump woman in her early fifties. Her clear complexion and fine features told of her former beauty which the hard life she endured could not efface completely. She was already mothering five children when her husband died in an accident at a construction site. She then remarried to a widower much older than herself, with his own set of children. With Isaac, her new husband, she had two more girls, Franka and Golde.

Like all the women of the older generation, Roise wore the traditional wig and was very observant. At the same time, she was quite liberal and understanding towards her children, who, like most of the young generation, were swept away by the secular tide. Thus she never got angry with them or criticized them harshly, but tried in her own motherly manner to teach them the proper way of living.

Franka's mother knew very well that Nohum and her daughter were going steadily. Whenever Franka was home with a cold or a spell of migraine, Nohum used to come over and sit at her bedside. Roise could not help but worry about her gentle daughter's future with a boy like Nohum. Though intelligent and well-mannered, and from a decent family, the young man was neither a businessman nor a good journeyman who could provide a living for a family. How then would these two manage to go on their own? she often wondered. Still, she knew her daughter's heart and was aware of the blossoming love between the two youngsters. She decided to be patient, wait and see how things will work out in due time.

When Nohum brought his books and a few of his belongings into the rented room, he was greatly surprised by what he saw and found there. The floor was freshly waxed in a shiny red colour; white sheets of paper covered the small kitchen stove in the corner, and the window was adorned with freshly washed half curtains. On the bed at the wall, the linen and pillow covers were white clean and the small table held a jug with fresh roses from the garden below. All this was Franka's handiwork and she herself soon appeared for the first good night kisses and embraces in her own house.

In the new lodging Nohum began to work in earnest on his autobiography. He would rise in the early hours of the morning and write undisturbed for an hour and a half or two, until it was time to rush home for breakfast and walk over to the workshop. The writing proceeded well; lines and paragraphs flowing freely as if from an inner fountain. Memoirs and episodes from his life, still fresh in his mind, were ordered into paragraphs and chapters. After three months, the first draft of his life story was ready. It had now to be copied in clear longhand and mailed to the YIVO Institute before the deadline. This was accomplished in a matter of weeks.

Soon after the completion of his autobiography, Nohum had to leave the room at Franka's place and return to his home. It was Sonia, Franka's older sister, who had intervened with her mother to get rid of the young tenant. Sonia was married but still at home, waiting to be joined with her husband, who was already several years in Palestine. As the oldest daughter, Sonia felt somehow responsible for her younger sister's behaviour. She was aware of Franka's late night visits into Nohum's upstairs room and had decided to put an end to this before it was too late.

Nohum returned to his stuffy and cluttered family room offended and disheartened. For the first time, doubts began to gnaw him about the future of his relationship with Franka. How could he continue to court her when he didn't earn enough to support himself or rent his own lodging? Nohum asked himself. He realized that he is only wasting his years at Sinai's workshop. He did not like at all this boot-stitching trade of his father and would, therefore, never learn it properly. Thus, he would never become financially independent like other young men of his age. What then would become of him and Franka? During many sleepless nights Nohum pondered over his condition with no plausible solution to be found. The only way out would be to emigrate to Palestine or America, where there seems to be a place for everyone.

Several years before, Franka's oldest brother married an American girl and went to live with her in New York. Now he writes that in due time he will be able to send the necessary papers and *shifcarten* for his parents and the two youngest sisters. And where is he in this scheme? Nohum thought. Besides, could he leave his own family, his hometown and his youth organization which he helped to build, and go overseas? All these questions and doubts hung over Nohum and Franka's future like a dark cloud on a clear horizon.

Still, they continued as before and even began to plan their first vacation trip together. During the summer, both of them were saving money and preparing the proper clothing for the trip, imagining the excitement of being alone and away from the familiar street and its people. The excursion was to begin in the first days of September and last for a week or more. They would travel by train to Warsaw and there embark on a steamboat on the Vistula to Casimir, a well-known picturesque town close to Cracow. There they would stay in a guest house, hiking in the area or resting at the shores of the Vistula.

Excitedly, the two young lovers awaited the arrival of September, a date destined to change their life and the lives of their people forever.

Chapter 26
WAR

Outside of Nohum and Franka's idyllic world, and quite
unnoticed by them, the clouds of war were gathering all during
the spring and summer of 1939. The Anschluss of Austria in 1938
was followed by the partition of Czechoslovakia in which Poland
and Hungary joined to share the spoils. Then came the German
demand for the return of Danzig and the Polish corridor that
divided the German mainland from Eastern Prussia. All of this
seemed still far off and unreal. All around were sure that Hitler
would not dare attack Poland and thus risk war with Britain and
France, Poland's guarantors. On Friday, September 1st, 1939, the
unbelievable did happen: the German motorized divisions and its
air force were let loose over Poland.

On that morning, Nohum awoke to the sound of the zooming
German fighter-planes that roamed unchallenged in the clear
September sky. Outside, on the street, there was panic and
pandemonium. From the houses around, people ran for shelter
into the vaulted gate of Nohum's courtyard. The place was full of
women and children, all trembling and crying aloud each time the
sound of shooting and bombing was heard from afar. When the
German bombers left, the townspeople learned that the Jewish
orphanage of the Centos Society was bombed, and that there are
many killed and wounded.

Together with Moshe Gelman, Nohum hurried to the scene of
the attack. Soon they reached the orphanage buildings tucked
away in a spacious villa behind Reymonta Street. Fire was still
smoldering in the ruins of the main building, around which
women and children ran calling for help. The hair and clothes of
some of them were singed and some were grovelling on the
ground. Killed and wounded were dragged from the buildings
and laid on the grass to await the arrival of medical help. A
doctor, wearing sandals and a housecoat, arrived in a droshky and
kneeled over a wounded woman. A nurse ran over to the doctor
screaming, "Panie doctor, the Director is wounded!" Beside the
veranda leading to the dining hall lay the maimed bodies of

children and a woman, still in her kitchen apron, with her legs stretched out and her head smashed. More droshkies arrived and Nohum and Moshe helped to carry the wounded, to be taken to the nearby military sanatorium. When the bombing was over, there were twelve dead and forty wounded, among them the director of the orphanage, a known Yiddish poet and educator.

Exhausted and deeply shaken, Nohum and Moshe left the place to return home. They crossed the railway tracks and proceeded along Parkowa Avenue towards Karczew Street. The highway above Karczew Street was overflowing with retreating soldiers and civilians. Buses, autos, and horse-driven carts cluttered the road, adding to the disarray and confusion. The men on foot were covered with sweat and dust; some of them resting with their bundles in the groves or open spaces on both sides of the road. Nohum and Moshe asked the reason of this exodus and were told that the radio had instructed all young men to leave Warsaw for the south, where a new defence line was to be formed. Warsaw itself was bombarded incessantly, whole blocks were on fire, and young and able bodied men were leaving the place.

At home, after supper, Moshe-Avrohom called Nohum aside and said, "Don't leave the house tonight, you'll help me bury our leather and valuables." After the other children left the restaurant for the room across the street, Nohum closed the shutters and doors in the front and back of the store and set out to work with his father. First they lifted several floor boards in the back room, behind the kitchen stove. Afterwards they took turns in digging a cavity in the ground beneath. The pit deepened and Nohum quietly carried out pails of sand into the courtyard. When the hole was deep enough, Moshe-Avrohom brought over from the room across the street several wrapped rolls of soft leather that he had bought lately to be used during the coming winter season in his shop. In addition, he brought a small wooden box with a few pieces of jewellery and family heirlooms. All these were carefully wrapped in sheets of paper and laid into the hiding. Soon the taken out boards were fitted back into the floor and nailed into its holding beams. The floor was then swept over with sand so no signs of the hiding should be left on the surface. All this time, father and son worked side by side without uttering a word. Suddenly, Moshe-Avrohom said:

'This war, Nohum, won't be like the last one. Not the same Germans. In a week or less they will be here. Save yourself, Nohum. Run to the east, like others. Old people, women and children, they may spare, but not you, a young man, and known in town as a Bundist."

"Where will I run, and how will I leave all of you?" Nohum answered, his voice choking with emotion.

"You are eighteen years old," Moshe-Avrohom replied. "A grown up man. Take your life in your hands and go!"

All through that night, Nohum weighed his father's words. He recalled the congested highway, full of retreating vehicles and people. Many of the refugees were hungry and exhausted, with no strength to continue. Some of them were on the way back to Warsaw and the towns around, telling horrifying stories of air bombardments, of dead men and horses all over the road. The German squadrons filled the Polish skies, bombarding and machine-gunning the runaways. How will he succeed in travelling hundreds of miles to the Rumanian or Russian border? And what would happen there to all this mass of people? And, above all, should he abandon his home and family, his beloved girl and his hometown, he, the revolutionary, the fighter for Jewish emancipation here, in the land where he was born and grew up...

Next morning, while Nohum was on the street in a long lineup for bread, several German fighter planes appeared on the horizon. Panic ensued; everyone ran for shelter in all directions. Instead of fleeing home, Nohum turned into the nearby Gorna Street, heading towards the wooded area of Pinai's large villa. There he fell to the ground beside the trunk of a thick tree, frightened by the rattle of the machine-guns and aerial cannons that filled the air. When he left the villa at last, after the bombers disappeared, he noticed a commotion in a small villa across the street. Nohum recognized the place; it was the residence of a Hasidic Rabbi who had resided for many years in Otwock. Nohum came closer and saw a group of Hasidim inside and outside the gate of the villa. A two-horse-drawn droshky, with its dark cover lifted, was waiting at the entrance, with the coachman on his elevated seat, ready for departure. Soon the Rebbe appeared, his face and beard covered with a red kerchief, his eyes sad and lowered. Behind him was his wife, her upper part of the body wrapped in a dark shawl. Two Hasidic lads carried leather suitcases which were laid on the droshky. The Hasidim crowded around the Rebbe, shaking his hand and taking leave of him.

"May God, His Name be Blessed, protect you, Rebbe! Pray for us. May the One Above have mercy upon us!" they murmured sadly. The Rebbe and his wife, with one companion, entered the droshky and hid under its dark covering. The driver whipped the horses and they galloped away. Some Hasidim left, others lingered around or returned to the Rebbe's house. Inside the gate stood an elderly woman who wept aloud: "The Rebbe left, woe is me! For twenty-five years my husband served him faithfully—and now he left. He'll be taken to America or Eretz Israel, and we'll remain here to die at the hands of the goyim, woe to us! We are left like lambs for the slaughter; only you, Master of the World, can save us!"

Shaken to his depths, Nohum left the place. On the way back, he passed the lane where the Youth-Bund organization was located. Since the fighting had started, the place was abandoned and empty. In a single day, the rich and complex infrastructure of organized Jewish life in Poland had fallen apart like a house of cards, and everybody was left to care for himself. Nohum unlocked the door and entered the local of the organization to which he devoted so much of his energy and skill. Had all this effort been worthwhile? he now wondered. The portraits of the two leaders of the Polish Bund looked down sadly from the pale and dust-covered frames. "Are they, too, running away, like the Rebbe, to save themselves, leaving the mass of Polish Jewry like sheep without a shepherd?" Nohum thought.

From the desk in the corner of the room, Nohum picked up the latest circular from the Central Committee of the Youth-Bund which had arrived several days before the outbreak of the war. He smiled bitterly when he read about the organizational measures to be taken in the event of war, such as replacing the local Youth Committees with girls, in case the boys were conscripted to the army. Now there was no local Youth Committee and, probably, no Central Committee either. None for all and everybody for himself, he thought bitterly. Soon he too, the Secretary of the Otwock Youth-Bund, would leave his family and comrades behind and run for safety to the East.

On the third day of the war, towards the evening, Nohum went over to Franka's place. In the backyard, at the water pump,

Nohum saw two men washing their faces and upper parts of their bodies under the cold stream of the pump. Nohum recognized Niuniek, the younger and taller man, Franka's brother-in-law. Only a year ago he had married Lonia, Franka's older sister, and they had settled nicely in a newly rented apartment in Warsaw. Niuniek was a construction carpenter from the city of Luck, in Volhynia, the Polish part of Western Ukraine. As many young men from the far province, he came to Warsaw and found there plenty of work in his trade. Here he also met and fell in love with Lonia. Once, it was in the spring, Nohum and Franka ventured to Warsaw to attend a performance of an operetta at the Yiddish theatre, and stayed overnight in Niuniek and Lonia's place.

The other man was a broad-shouldered fellow in his forties, with a stern waxen face of a recluse. He introduced himself to Nohum as Abrasha, Niuniek's neighbour in the Warsaw apartment. Both men, together with Lonia and Franka's younger sister, Golde, just arrived on foot from Warsaw. They had walked all day, amidst air attacks and bombardments, and encountered terrifying scenes of death and destruction all the way along. Soon Franka came out carrying a large bowl of warm water and placed it on the ground, beside the wooden bench, under a young acacia tree. The men sat down, removed their shoes, and soaked their sore feet for some time. Soon Nohum joined them in the glass-covered veranda where tea and cake were served. At the table, Niuniek and Abrasha began to discuss further plans of their flight. They would leave Lonia here, with her family, and continue alone to the east, for Niuniek's hometown Luck. Abrasha spread out a small map of Poland and dotted the route of their escape. They would try to reach Lublin by one of the refugee trains that passes the Otwock station. From there, they would continue, by train or otherwise, to Chelm, and then cross the Bug River. From there one can speedily reach Brest-Litowsk and the city of Luck.

"We can not wait, Niuniek," Abrasha pleaded. "The Germans are surrounding Warsaw, and may arrive in Otwock any day. It will be too late then..."

Niuniek sat silently, his hands framing his head, and looked painfully at Lonia and the rest around. Beside him, Lonia gently patted his dark hair and encouraged him to go.

"You must run, Niuniek. All young men are supposed to leave for the East. In a week or so you will join your mother and brothers in Luck. Don't worry for me. I'm here with my parents. Anyway, I'll join you afterwards. Leave it to me, I'll find you wherever you'll be."

"I'll join you," Nohum said suddenly. "Will you let me go with you? I won't be a burden... You'll see..." Everybody around the table fell silent. Abrasha looked at Nohum intensively, as if weighing in his mind the worthiness of this unexpected companion.

"I'll leave it to Niuniek," he finally said. "If he agrees, I'm not against it."

As all eyes turned to Niuniek, Franka moved over to him, laid her hand on his shoulders, and said:

"Take Nohum with you, Niuniek. He's smart and brave and he'll make a good companion."

"Agreed," Niuniek interrupted his silence. "We are leaving, the three of us, tomorrow night. We have a full day to rest and prepare ourselves. Tomorrow night..."

Elated by Niuniek's decision, Nohum got up and shook hands with Niuniek and Abrasha. Soon he left and Franka walked him out of the house. They entered the empty courtyard across the street and there, behind a thick pine tree, embraced and showered each other with kisses.

"I am leaving you, Franka, I'm running away..." Nohum whispered.

"Go, Nohum. Don't hesitate. I'll come later. I'll join Lonia and come with her to Luck."

"I too have an inner feeling that we'll meet again, that you'll be mine forever..."

Next morning, Nohum notified his parents that he is leaving at night, with two other men, for Luck, in the Ukraine. Moshe-Avrohom, bent over his sewing machine, lifted his head and nodded approvingly. Itte, however, broke out in bitter sobbing.

"Nohumel, my child," she lamented, "where are you running, in the midst of the war? Who will care for you? What will become of you? Woe is me!"

"Let him go," Moshe-Avrohom said sternly. "He's going with two grown-ups who know their way about. Soon we'll hear from him from Luck."

Itte quietened down and began to assist Nohum in preparing his knapsack with a few shirts, socks and underwear, as well as a food package for the first day of his voyage. Nohum searched his drawer where he kept his writing books with poems and stories and the handwritten copy of his autobiography. He decided to leave all his writing at home, and picked up only a few photographs of his family, Shaindel and Franka. He then went over to the restaurant, and from 'there to the courtyard, taking leave from all those dear and familiar places where he spent his childhood and adolescent years.

Towards the evening, all the inhabitants of the courtyard learned about Nohum's departure and many came out to take leave of him and wish him well. It was a warm September evening, and most of the people preferred to congregate outside than to stay in their darkened and stuffy homes. Itte walked around the place weeping and wringing her hands. Over and over she embraced Nohum, kissed his face and head, and her hot tears came down like raindrops over his face.

"Where are you leaving me, my Kaddish, my only treasure?" she wept and trembled. Then, raising her eyes, she asked, "What will become of us, Master of the World? Why are you punishing us so much?" Around her were Nohum's three younger sisters and little brother Godel, all of them clinging to him lovingly, touching his hands, and all of them in tears. Finally, Nohum went over to say goodbye to his father. Moshe-Avrohom was, as always, quiet and composed. Only his eyes had a deep and immense sadness and his countenance seemed more dim and clouded. Without a word, he handed over Nohum a ten zlotys bill and embraced him.

"May God protect you, Nohum," he whispered. "Remain a Jew, wherever...And remember us... remember..."

Nohum tore himself away from his father and walked to the gate of the courtyard. Here he turned around and waved to all a last time. Then, hurriedly, he went through the gate and began walking upwards the quiet and darkened Swiderska Street to Franka's house. Outside the wooden fence was Franka, waiting for him, together with Pinie Cukerkop, who had come over to take leave of Nohum.

"You are late, Nohum!" Franka exclaimed. "Niuniek and Abrasha left half an hour ago for the train station."

Hurriedly, Nohum with Franka and Pinie at his side, proceeded down the street towards the railway station. Passing by, Nohum once more glanced at Itchele Einfeld's two storey apartment house where he grew up. It was late, and Nohum decided against entering once more into the courtyard. The train may leave any minute and he'll be left without his comrades. Soon Nohum and his companions were under the railway tunnel and into the large square in front of the darkened station. Approaching the station by the left side sidewalk, they noticed a long passenger train, fully packed with people. They entered the empty, unattended platform and began to walk along the cars, calling in hushed voices for Niuniek and Abrasha. Suddenly, Abrasha squeezed his head out of an open window and called: "Here we are. Push in, latecomer."

Standing on the step of the car, Nohum embraced first Pinie and then Franka. "My one and only, let's hope we'll meet again." Nohum said as he kissed her. He then squeezed into the dark mass of people that filled the compartment and found his way beside Niuniek and Abrasha. All sat silently, in the dark, waiting for the train to leave. It was early morning when the locomotive gave out a prolonged whistle and the train began to move. As he looked through the window, Nohum thought for a moment that he saw his father, Moshe-Avrohom, with his sister, Tema, at father's side. Both were standing on the empty platform looking helplessly towards him. Nohum wanted to call out to them but no sound came forth from his throat. The train was moving faster and in a second the image of his father and sister disappeared.

Was it really his father who hurried at dawn with his older daughter, to send her, too, away with Nohum, or only a frightful mirage, the product of his heightened imagination? Nohum would never know. Through the open window he now recognized the outlines of the familiar villas and hotel buildings along Warszawska Street and beyond, on the road to Srodborow.

Nohum repeated to himself as the train carried him further and further away from home into the war-torn world:

"Goodbye my family!
Goodbye Swiderska Street!
Goodbye my hometown!
Goodbye!"